DANCING WITH TEMPTATION

BARRE TO BAR
BOOK TWO

SUMMER COOPER

LOVY BOOKS

Roxie

"Well, this just sucks," Roxie whispered then turned over in the bed, away from the last man she'd ever wanted to sleep with. Again.

Her eyelids closed as the blue orbs rolled around in their sockets. Had she really been this stupid? She opened her eyes quickly to see gray light glancing off the walls. They were familiar but not the walls she'd have found in her own bedroom. It was almost impossible not to groan out loud, not when being faced with that much truth.

Oh yes. It was true, no matter how much of a mistake she knew it was.

She'd slept with Lincoln Young.

Holy fucking moly.

Heat flooded through her body, shame mixed with pleasure because it might have been vanilla sex, but it had been damned good. Memories of the sounds she'd made, how she begged him for more, made her body pulse into aroused life. But they also made her brain twitch with…embarrassment? Was that it? She was embarrassed and not really ashamed?

"Are you going to sneak out and pretend this didn't happen?" Lincoln's far-too-sexy voice nearly made her jump out of the bed. It was early Saturday morning and they'd spent the entire night exploring every inch of each other's bodies. Why was he awake?

"Oh, you're awake?" She sat up and pulled the covers up over her chest. That was a stupid move, he'd seen everything she had to offer already, and she wasn't really the modest kind of person, but…yeah. The need to protect herself from him in all ways was still there. She wouldn't poke at what all of those ways were Too much though.

"Let's get one thing straight, Link." She pretended not to notice how he cringed when she used the nickname, even if it did give her a small bit of pleasure to see his annoyance. "That was just a…"

"Mistake?" He offered, interrupting her. She didn't look at him this time but stared at the wall ahead of her instead.

"Yeah, something like that. I still hate you, you know?" A shrug of her shoulders made the bedding slip and she quickly pulled it back up. "Rebound sex you could call it. Or my boyfriend called me a whore and broke up with me and I needed friend sex. Whatever. It doesn't matter to me what you call it. So long as you don't call me for it again. It was like the last time…"

The words 'that night of the fire that killed my parents' almost passed her lips, but she cut them off.

"I understand." He answered, a chuckle in his voice. That sound of mirth annoyed her a little, but she let it go. If she said something he might stop climbing out of bed.

Roxie averted her gaze as he walked out of the bedroom naked. Well, she did until he was past her, and then she watched him walk away, her eyes hungrily taking in the powerful swimmer's body that had fascinated her even when they were teenagers.

It wasn't like she'd admit that to anyone, however. Especially not to him.

"Are you going to stay for breakfast?" He called out before he went into the bathroom.

"No, um, I'll crash at a friend's place." She called out, not sure which friend that might be, but she'd figure something out.

The second the shower came on, she ordered an Uber, hopped out of the bed, and dug around in her bag for a change of clothes. When she had something picked out, she walked to another bathroom, showered, and went back to his room to get her bag. She had on a black tank top, short denim shorts, and light blue deck shoes. No socks. The damn things made her feel like she was smothering when she had them on.

Normally she'd dry her hair and put on makeup before she'd walk out the door, but not today. She just wanted out of Lincoln's presence. Thankfully, the Uber arrived before he could come out of the house to ask her another embarrassing question. Like, do you want to go back to my room for another round of awesome, mind-blowing sex that you won't be able to wash out of your memory, no matter how hard you try to scrub it away?

Her cheeks were red again and she hated it. She'd had a lot of sex in her life, it wasn't anything she was ashamed of, but for some reason, sex with Lincoln had been different.

"Can you take me to a hotel, please?" She asked the female driver, a pretty Hispanic woman with a cheerful smile. Roxie's nails tapped against her teeth as she watched the car pull away from the security gate. Hurry, please...

"Which one, miss?" The woman asked and Roxie shrugged again.

"The Pelican Inn, that'll be fine." Roxie decided finally with a nod.

"Cool, no problem." The driver said and pulled out into traffic.

Roxie dug her phone out of her back pocket and stared at the screen. She had over thirty missed calls and voice messages. What the fuck?

A quick scroll showed that most of the calls were from Wendy or Nathan. Hearing anything from the man that had called her a whore wasn't high on her list of things to do so Roxie opened Wendy's messages first.

Wendy said to call her at any time, just to let her know how Roxie was, so she hit the dial button to call her friend.

"Hey," Wendy said before the first ring had even finished. She must have been sitting there with her phone in her hands.

"Hey, everything's alright," Roxie said, not wanting to give too much away to the driver. The woman looked nice enough, but she was a stranger.

"There's been some shady-looking mofos hanging around since you left. One of the thug-looking bastards even came in and asked me where Nathan was." Wendy sighed, her way of showing how annoyed she was.

"Sorry about that." Roxie soothed, her lips stretched in a smile at her friend. "Has he been around?"

"No, not that I've seen. Where did you stay last night?" Wendy asked in a tone meant to convey total innocence, but Roxie knew better.

"Cow." She said as an answer, knowing Wendy would take it all in fun. "I stayed at Lincoln's. If you *must* know."

"Oh, but I must. The man shows up, punches out your now ex-boyfriend, and takes off with you. Did you sleep with Prince Charming, master of all things manly, by any chance?" Wendy's tone told Roxie she already knew the answer to that, purely speculation, but it was hard to deny the truth.

"That's nunya, my friend. None ya business." Roxie laughed and stared out the back window of the Honda the driver had picked her up in.

"That means yes, then. Listen, I don't want to upset you, but I don't think you should come back here for a while. Find somewhere to lie low. At least until these creepy fuckers stop coming around. If you need something let me know and I'll bring it to you." Wendy's normally cheery voice turned serious and Roxie breathed in again, a little overwhelmed suddenly.

But she'd been in worse situations than this. It wasn't a new position for her to be in at all. "Will do. I may need some more clothes, but I think I took everything he hadn't destroyed."

Which might have been admitting more than she wanted to, but something told Roxie the driver had probably heard and seen worse. It was Myrtle Beach after all. A lot of strange things happened here.

"That bastard," Wendy whispered over the line. "I'll go up and go through what's left. Hopefully, some of your designer stuff survived."

Designer clothes, even super-expensive designer clothes, were the least of Roxie's worries, but she didn't say it out loud.

"Okay, listen, I'm almost at the hotel. I'm headed over to the Pelican. I'll get settled in there and then message you, alright?"

"Sounds good, sister. Don't forget to buzz me, okay?" Wendy's sweet voice, always so ready to laugh, was serious again and Roxie hated Nathan for making her friend worry like that.

"I will, I promise. Love ya." Roxie offered, something she rarely said to anyone, but she felt that Wendy needed to know it right now.

"I love you too, Rox, take care, babe," Wendy said and hung up.

"Rough night?" The driver asked, without an ounce of judgment.

"Men, what can I tell you?" Roxie gave her third shrug of the day and tried not to meet the woman's eyes. Roxie hated pity.

"I know a safe place, if you need one, that's the only reason I asked. If you need to disappear, honey, I know just the place for you."

"I don't think I'm in that bad of a situation that I

need to disappear just yet." She started to say, but decided not to turn down an opportunity that she might need later. She had learned that a long time ago. "Do you have a card, though?"

"I sure do, I'll get one for you when we get to the hotel."

"Awesome." Roxie nodded and went quiet.

The drive took ten more minutes, but the woman was soon parked and handing Roxie a card. She smiled over her shoulder at Roxie, no pity in sight. "Call me anytime, even if you don't have money for a ride, if you need out of a bad situation."

"I wouldn't do that." Roxie protested. "I mean, not pay you that is. This is how you make money, after all."

"I know, but sisters have to look out for each other, right?" The woman's head tilted and Roxie looked away, down at the card in her hands. Lily Gonzales, that was her name.

"Thanks, Lily. That's awesome, really," Roxie finally answered and opened the door. "I guess I need to check-in, oh, here."

Roxie tapped the app on her phone to pay Lily and added a tip. She'd leave a review after she checked in.

"Thanks," Lily said and waited for Roxie to get out of the car.

"Thank you," Roxie replied before she closed the door. She waved as the woman drove away and then headed into the reception area of the small hotel. It was an old place, built in the sixties if the interior was anything to judge by, but it was clean and cheap, which was why Roxie knew about it. She hadn't always had enough money to afford a place on her own.

The hotel was close to a shopping plaza and had a restaurant on the other side of the parking lot. It was suitable as a home, for now. As she walked into her room a little while later, she wondered for the first time how Lincoln had known to show up at her place. He'd just…appeared. She'd ask him later. Like on Monday, when she went to work. Calling him now would just bring that heat back to her cheeks.

Which reminded her, she still had to deal with all of the Nathan messages. She didn't want to, but curiosity wouldn't let her ignore his calls. She threw her bag down, flopped down on the bed, and took out her phone.

"I knew you were a fucking whore. I knew you'd move on the minute you found some rich guy to fuck your brains out. I don't know how I was stupid enough to think you were good enough for me. Fuck you, Roxie. I hope you catch an STD." Nathan's angry but still petulant voice spewed from her phone's speaker.

Roxie rolled her eyes and played the next one. It wasn't like she'd never been called a whore before. Whatever.

"You're nothing but a gold-digging bitch. Fuck you." He was still angry in that one too.

There were more messages, messages she should probably ignore, but she didn't. She was made of stronger stuff than the idiot gave her credit for.

"I'm sorry, Rox. I was mad. I know you aren't a whore. I know you're probably pissed at me, but I really need that money. Can you get 100K from one of your rich friends? Maybe that Emily woman? Or even eighty? Hell, even fifty or thirty thousand dollars would do it. I just need to get these guys off my back. Please? Let me know. Um, yeah. Bye." He hadn't sounded so sure in that last call.

Roxie saw there was one more call and took a deep breath before she hit play.

"Fuck you, Roxie. Get me that money however you have to, you fucking slut or you'll wish you had. Don't push me, Rox. Or you'll be in a whole lot of trouble, baby."

Now, what the fuck did he mean there? Roxie frowned up at the white popcorn ceiling trying to work out what exactly Nathan had meant. She'd be in a whole lot of trouble? For what?

Probably some dream he'd had while he was high, she finally decided and put the phone down. People that snorted opioids weren't always the most reliable, nor were people that added alcohol to those pills.

She'd found a few of the illicit pills scattered around her apartment over the last year and there'd been more there tonight. She'd scooped them up and flushed them before the cops came in, so she wouldn't get in trouble.

There was only one person that could have dropped the pills and that was Nathan.

Bastard.

Roxie blew air out of her nose, got up, and messaged Wendy.

"I'm at the hotel, got a room, going to the shops to buy a few things." Read the message she sent to her friend.

Wendy sent back a thumb's up. "The designer stuff is fine, he probably wanted to sell it. There's a few more things. I'll bring them by whenever."

"Great. I'll let you know. Going out now." Roxie sent back and grabbed her handbag from the bigger bag she had some of her stuff stored in.

Going out might not be a good idea, not when thugs were hanging around her apartment and Nathan was vacillating between wanting to kill her and begging her for money, but she couldn't stay cooped up. Walking would help relieve some of the anxiety that made her want to pace. She'd get something to eat at the restaurant before she went, she decided, though. Being around other anonymous people over a plate of sausage, gravy, and biscuits was something else that would soothe her nerves.

Roxie smiled at a red-head waitress named Pam, or so her badge read, as she walked in, and then went to sit in a booth in the corner of the restaurant. She had a view of the entire parking lot from there. She'd see anyone that came near the restaurant or the hotel.

"Orange juice, coffee, and the special, please," Roxie said as the waitress walked up, a smile on her pretty face.

"Very good. Want anything extra with it?" The woman offered but Roxie shook her head.

"No, that'll be fine." And she hoped it was. Life had suddenly turned upside down. Again. What a fucking mess.

2

Roxie

*L*ife had become incredibly confusing since Lincoln Young walked back into her life, Roxie decided. She looked around the house he'd asked her to decorate, wondering what else life had in store for her. Some peace and quiet wouldn't be a bad thing, that was for sure.

"Thanks for coming over," Lincoln said as he came into the kitchen to stand across from her.

He didn't come close to her or try to kiss her. She wasn't sure what to expect when she got his message to come by his place. She'd been in the process of getting her car from Wendy, wondering if she should call Emily or any of her other friends, and basically just being numb from the events of the last 24 hours.

With her hands wrapped around her elbows, Roxie turned to face the last man she wanted to talk to right now. At the moment, being anywhere near him felt like her emotions were a sore tooth that her tongue wouldn't stay away from. Yet, she had to be here, she had to face him.

"What can I do for you, Lincoln?" She moved, her arms out by her side now instead of closed around her middle, and took a seat at the table. Her blue gaze followed him to the chair he took across from her.

"Well, you're done with the house now and I have enough help at work now that Tanya has moved down here with the company…." His voice trailed off in a way that made Roxie's eyes narrow.

"So, you're laying me off? No problem." She paused to take a deep breath, trying not to panic because it was actually a huge problem. "I can find work somewhere else."

"No, that's not what I was getting at." Lincoln was the one who sighed this time, his brown eyes troubled and looking for a safe place to land.

"Are you blushing?" She asked before she could clamp down on the question.

"Probably. Look, I've never done this kind of thing before," he spit out but finally met her eyes. "I want you to teach me how to use that room upstairs."

"Oh?" She wasn't sure whether it was a surprise or a question. Maybe both.

"I have no experience in this area, Roxie." His voice still didn't sound comfortable saying her chosen name, but he'd learned to use it instead of the name she'd been given at birth, at least.

"Alright. And you want me to - what? Take money for sex?" She was about to be really pissed off, but he jumped in again to deny the question.

"No, Roxie. Fuck no!" He shot up out of the chair and started to pace the length of the kitchen. "I want you to teach me how to be…whatever that room entails. Whatever makes your brain tick in that world as you see it."

His words faltered as he fought to find the right ones that wouldn't offend her and still get his point across. His hands waved at the room, his eyes flitting between her and the ceiling of the kitchen.

"I see." She murmured, her elbows on the table, hands clasped together. Rather than getting angry, she waited for him to finish, slightly amused at his discomfort. "You want me to teach you to be a dom?"

She sucked at her teeth, trying not to laugh at his discomfort. It would be rude to laugh at him and she knew it. Laughing might also put him off the idea and lead to him going about all of this the wrong way. "Or do you want me to teach you to be a sub, Lincoln?"

"What?" He looked at her now, his eyes narrowed in confusion.

"Well." She got up from the chair and walked closer to him, following him every time he took a step back. He eventually backed right up against the wall, his hands flat against the smooth surface. "Do you want to be the one doing the spanking, Lincoln, or do you want to be the one getting spanked?"

She let the fingers of her right hand dance up his abdomen, over his chest, until she reached his chin, her index finger tapping there until he looked down at her. His nostrils were flared, his pupils dilating and retracting as thoughts flitted through his brain. "Which one is it that you want me to teach you, Lincoln?"

"I want you to teach me everything, Roxie. Everything you know." His voice was low, rough with desire, and she couldn't deny the way her body responded.

Heat flushed into her cheeks and her lips as she leaned closer into him, her chest against his as her face tilted up for a kiss she couldn't deny herself. But she paused, waiting for something she couldn't name. "Everything?"

"All of it," Lincoln muttered as he wrapped his arms around her waist to pull her close just as his lips dropped down that fraction of an inch to meet hers at last.

Memories of the night before, of just how good that

plain old vanilla sex had been with him, flooded into her mind. He'd made her feel a million different things last night, things she didn't want to think about, but couldn't stop herself from wanting. Her fingers clenched at his shoulders, drawing him closer while her tongue ran out of her mouth to meet his.

He tasted of coffee and cinnamon, but it was the feel of his soft lips against hers, the silky slide of his tongue that made her moan and forget what he'd asked of her. She could feel how aroused he was, and it only made her hungry for more. She'd denied she'd ever been attracted to him, had pretended she didn't remember that night they'd spent together when she was eighteen, but she could still feel those first touches as if they were scars that her skin couldn't forget. Ten years had passed since that night, but her body couldn't forget him. Especially when she'd...

"Roxie." His lips slid away from hers to moan her name, his fingers digging into her as if to draw her even closer to him.

Holy fucking shit, she had to stop this, she thought, as a figurative bucket of cold water rushed over her. Distance, she needed miles of distance between her body and his if she was going to think. She needed to be far away from the hunger in his eyes, though she knew she wasn't going to get more than a few feet of relief.

"No, stop, Lincoln." She held a hand up as she walked

back to the table. "I'm sorry, we have to discuss this rationally. I shouldn't have started that."

"I'm…what?" He scrubbed at his dark hair with strong fingers, his face contorted with surprise. "I'm sorry, have I done something wrong?"

"Not at all." She protested quickly, sitting down in the chair she'd vacated earlier. "We just need to do this rationally. We need to discuss a contract."

"A contract?" Lincoln scoffed, laughter dancing in his eyes until he saw how seriously she stared at him. "Oh, you're serious?"

"I am, yes. People pay a lot of money for this kind of education, Lincoln. And if it's to be done safely and satisfactorily, we need a contract." She stared up at him calmly, not concerned at all about the consequences of being so intimately entwined with his education into her world.

She needed the money; he wanted an education. Sure, she could have offered one of the other girls the chance to teach Lincoln about her world, could have given them the opportunity to make some money, but for old time's sake, she'd teach him. And with a contract in place, neither one of them would break the rules, not without breaking the contract and ending the whole deal.

She could keep him at arm's length, even with sex involved, as long as there was a contract in place.

Besides, it would give them both a goal to work towards, put in place the rules they should both follow, and give her a sense of security. Sex would not be mentioned in said contract, because she did not fuck men for money. She fucked them because she wanted to, because it was part of the training, not because of the money. She'd had clients that she never had intercourse with, while with others she had. It depended on the client, on her own wishes, and what was in the contract.

In all her years in this life, she'd never broken a contract once. Clients had crossed lines a time or two, some had asked to end the contract early when someone else caught their attention, but that was part of the beauty of the contract. It kept her heart and emotions out of the business arrangement.

"A contract? Alright. What would that look like? What would be in it?" He sat down across from her again, his desire under control. Good, she noted with a slight smile.

"First, payment will be specified. This is a business arrangement, if you can agree to that then we can continue." She paused, caught his eyes before she carried on. "Sex is up to me, not to you. If, *if* I decide to have sex with you during the contract, then you will ensure we are both protected against pregnancy and STDs."

Unlike the night before, she thought as her face blanched. Hopefully, she wouldn't find herself with even more problems as a result of that night. She'd taken her birth control pill, so hopefully, that would protect her from pregnancy, at least.

"You mean I have to use condoms?" He asked with a nod. "I have no problem with that. Or with agreeing to whatever terms you set."

"Don't be so quick to give in, Lincoln. This is a negotiation. I'll be asking for more than you're paying me now, for instance. You have to be sure you're getting your money's worth out of the deal." She smiled at him, knowing he'd agree to whatever she demanded. He wouldn't have asked her to teach him anything if he hadn't wanted her as more than his PA.

So long as their relationship remained secured in a contract, she'd give him everything he wanted and more. Maybe life would return to normal after the contract ended, which reminded her. "How long do you want me for?"

"I, what?" He was confused again, his brows together.

"How long do you want the contract to last? A month? A few months? A year?"

"I don't know. I hadn't thought about that, really." His gaze became distant, as if he was considering how long it would take to get her out of his system.

"Alright, how about I print out one of my generic contracts and you can look it over, see what you want to change before we go any further? There's a printer in your office. I'll just send one from my cloud to the printer and you can look it over." She held up her phone and he nodded.

"That sounds good." He breathed a sigh of relief that she heard, even if he tried to hide it behind his hand as she left the room.

There was a bounce to her step as she walked into his office to retrieve the papers she'd already sent to the printer. This might not be a good idea, but she needed work. Work that wouldn't have her out in the public eye and was...private. Privacy was paramount in arrangements like this, by nature. Although the contract would not be notarized, she would be able to use it if problems arose later, not that she thought Lincoln would become problematic, but still. The protection was there if she needed it because she'd learned long ago not to always trust people. People broke your heart and bled you dry if you let them.

A contract with Lincoln would be a solution to her money problems and her need to be out of the limelight while Nathan was on the run, hiding from people that were after him and her too, if the things Wendy had said meant anything.

Wendy had brought her car over earlier, along with her bike, worried the whole time that she'd been followed. She was nearly in tears by the time Roxie poured her into a cab and assured her everything would be alright. Roxie wouldn't let her friend worry that she'd led those fucking thugs to Roxie's door.

The security fence around the place and the presence of another human being might protect her while she was with Lincoln, but she still had to be careful, she decided as she walked back into the kitchen. But first, he had to be aware of exactly what was going on. She was the one that sighed this time, sitting across from him with the papers in her right hand.

"Before I give you these papers, do you understand that Nathan is still out there, that he's threatening me, and that there are men after him that might just be after me as well?" Her left eyebrow lifted but he only smiled back at her.

"I know that, Roxie. I, uh, I had a guy watching your place last night. That's how I knew you were in trouble." He confessed, reminding her that she'd meant to ask him that very question.

"Oh, right. Well, that brings me to question two. Do you understand that Nathan or those other people might also be after you because of me?" She didn't hesitate to ask.

"Of course." He answered quickly with a nod of his head. "I know what I'm getting into, Roxie. I'm not a complete innocent in all things."

"Alright. Have a read of this then. Keep in mind, it's generic, you can add or take away whatever you like. I'll have a read over what you propose later, and then we'll go from there." She handed him a pen from her bag and stood up. "I packed everything into my car before I came over, in case Nathan or the goons followed Wendy to my place. I didn't want anything else of mine being destroyed. I'm going to grab a couple of bags to leave here if that's alright with you? I know they'll be safe here."

"That's fine." He mumbled, his eyes on the papers, his finger tapping the pen against his lips as he read. At least he was taking it seriously, she thought as she left the room and headed out the back door. The day was warm already, but the breeze off the ocean was nice.

Roxie stood on the porch looking out beyond the security fence. She could just see over the top of it and spotted waves crashing against the shore. Not a bad place to hide out, even if she had to teach the man inside how to use a room he'd asked her to create. It might be fun, it usually was, and at least she kind of liked Lincoln. Even if he'd teased her mercilessly when they were kids.

That was a million years and a hundred lifetimes ago, or so it felt. He wasn't the same boy he'd been back then, and she certainly wasn't the same girl. She could treat this as nothing more than it was; a business arrangement. Which reminded her, he had a man keeping an eye on her last night. That meant she'd get security as well as money out of the arrangement. She dismissed the small alarm she felt over knowing he'd had security watching her all this time. That's how Lincoln operated, keeping people around him safe. And, if he proved a worthy student, she might get some good sex out of it as well. Not a bad arrangement at all, really.

3

Lincoln

"I don't understand what this is, Roxie." Lincoln put the papers down on his kitchen table and stared at her in the morning sunlight.

The purple hadn't washed out of her hair yet, he noticed, when the sunlight turned the strands into amethyst slivers. He liked it, even if it was unconventional for most of the women he'd spent time with in the past. But it was just another thing to like about her.

Her wry smile shouldn't be infectious, but still, he smiled back as he looked at her.

"Then I'll explain it to you." She took the collection of papers from the table and started on page one. "Here we name ourselves, the length of the contract, and what terms are acceptable for breaking the contract."

"Such as?" He asked blandly, trying to sound as nonchalant as she did.

"Do you mean the acceptable conditions for breaking the contract early?" She shrugged and glanced up at him to catch his nod before looking back down at the papers. "You don't like the way I teach, for example. Or you find someone you want to be faithful to, or you just get bored with the whole thing. I will be paid in full, however, no matter the conditions. Once you sign this, you owe me the full payment."

"Alright." He agreed with a nod of his head. Money was no object for him. He'd pay her whatever she asked. "What else?"

Roxie paused to write something into the margin of one paragraph before she continued. "How long do you want this contract to last?"

"How long do they usually last?" He rebutted, wondering how many times she'd had this conversation. He wasn't judging her. It was simple curiosity that made him wonder.

"Some last six months, some one or two months. It depends on what *you* want, Lincoln." She tapped the pen against the papers now, a sign that she was agitated.

That amused him for reasons he didn't really want to examine for now, so he just gave a slight nod. "Alright, how about one month with an option to renew?"

This time she nodded her head as she wrote something under another paragraph. "That will work. Now, about the reasons I can break the contract..."

"Oh, we can both break it?" The dark eyebrows above his brown eyes lifted while his eyelids opened a little wider.

"Of course. I won't tolerate abuse of any kind, emotional, physical, verbal. That's my number one deal-breaker. Not that I'm saying you would do any of that, but it's best to have it in the open from the start I've learned. I've had to break contracts before." This time, Roxie didn't look at him. Her mouth was set in a grim line, but the rest of her face was hidden.

She'd been hurt before and that made him want to punch whoever it was that had hurt her. He'd known all those years ago that the girl he knew as Chloe wasn't prepared to live in the world she'd escaped to, but she'd survived this long. She'd even succeeded in that world until her boyfriend had burned down the place that had given her that success. There had to be stories for her to tell and stories she'd probably keep hidden away forever. He wouldn't push her to talk though, no matter how much he wanted to do just that.

"The rest itemizes what you want, and here you don't have to be detailed, but it would be good if you could describe how you'd like me to dress, even my hair color if you want me to change that. I'm not your slave during this contract, but I will be what you want me to be. You will cover the costs of whatever changes I have to make." She paused, pursed her lips, as she read the next paragraph. "You also have to put down things that you want me to teach you, if you have ideas, and things you will absolutely not participate in."

"Such as?" He asked again, just to hear her response. He knew exactly what he would and would not participate in just fine. He wasn't totally sheltered from the world of sex.

"Group sex, anal, either receiving or giving, rape play for my part. That's a hard no for me." Her lips pursed again when she saw his confusion. "Some men really do take this as a contract to make me their slave. They think they can ignore the rules and have been known to cause a lot of damage. Rape play is not something I will take part in, even when you take total control. If I use the safe word, you have to stop, no matter what stage of sex or playtime we're in. I don't care if your balls turn black and fall off, if I use that safe word, you'd better stop whatever you're doing if you want to keep your family jewels."

The hard note in her voice made something ache deep in his chest. Was she speaking from experience or just knowledge of what could happen if she wasn't as hard as a diamond? Fuck, this was more complicated than he'd thought it would be when he asked her to bring him into her world. Contracts and safe words weren't quite what he'd had in mind, but it was obvious she needed this if she was to do what he asked. That was the only reason he'd agreed, he'd seen how serious she was when she mentioned the contract and he couldn't argue with her.

If she needed this to feel safe, he'd give her a dozen contracts.

"Agreed." He said when he realized the silence had stretched out too long. "I won't do anything you don't want me to do."

"Good. Now, the rest is just arranging dates if you have something specific in mind, renewal agreements, things like that." Lincoln could see the way her shoulder relaxed as she moved on through the contract, the hard part must be over with.

She wrote a few more things into the margins of the contract as they moved along, and he waited for her to tell him what came next.

"I like to be paid in cash, upfront. Once you write what you want into the contract, I'll type it up and we can begin on whichever date you specify."

"Okay. Well, as soon as possible. Paying upfront is no problem, and I don't want you to change anything about yourself, Roxie. I may buy you outfits, other things, but I don't want you to become a living form of a blowup doll. I like you too much as you are." He realized he'd said too much when her left eyebrow quirked up in shocked amusement.

He quickly moved his gaze to the landscape outside, or rather the seascape, and tried not to feel like an idiot about to have sex for the first time. Which reminded him… "Will we be having sex?"

"Eventually, perhaps. If you just want a prostitute, I can give you the contact details of several I know. I'm not a prostitute, Lincoln." She moved closer to turn his face back to her, obviously wanting to ensure he understood. "The sex part is now and will always be my choice. Of course, you have a say if you don't want sex as well, but having sex is ultimately my choice if we get to that point. My lifestyle isn't just about sex, you see. It's about gratification of all types."

"I see." He *didn't* quite see it all just yet but knew she'd guide him. "This is all new for me, I don't wish to offend you. I would never hurt you, either. I just want to be as clear as you are."

"It's alright." She took a deep breath, looked down at her hands as if searching for the answer to life, something she might find if she squinted hard enough, but looked up again finally. "I know you're new to this. I'm assuming you've continued to have sex and have some ideas of what you want to learn?"

"I didn't become a priest after you left that morning, no." Fuck, this was weird, he couldn't help but think. He was usually the one in control, the one giving orders, but right now he felt like a schoolboy caught fibbing about how much he'd studied. "I have ideas, things I want to explore with you."

Talking about these things was hard, but he knew if he didn't, he'd never get what he'd paid for. He chewed at his lower lip unconsciously, deep in thought. How to say exactly what he wanted? Was he even really sure he knew what he wanted?

"To explore until I find what blows my mind, that's all I can say at the moment." His eyes found hers and their gazes locked. "How do we do that?"

"We start with a snazzy little quiz you can find online. It looks stupid, some of it is downright horrifying, but it'll give us an idea of what you really want. Give me your phone." She held out her hand, her face expectant. He couldn't resist. "This site is one of the few I trust in the world of kink. It will tell us what you hate and what you love. It's long so I'll make some phone calls while you go through it."

"Oh, what if I don't know what something is?" He had a feeling there would be quite a few of those situations.

"I won't be far away. Come find me." She gave him a pert wink before she got up and left the kitchen.

"Right, go find her. Or I can just look it up." He

muttered as he started the anonymous 'How kinky are you' quiz.

As he poked at answers and read the questions, Lincoln's jaw dropped and closed at least a dozen times. All the questions were exceptionally personal, but he could see the point now that he was fifty questions in. It wasn't a 'Which animal were you in a previous life' kind of quiz. It was meant to help the respondent find out what they should explore.

Lincoln ticked the box for bondage but had to look up what some of the answers under the question about rope play meant. He had no clue what shibari was, for instance, but when he looked it up decided he wanted to know more about it. Some of the other questions were as bad as Roxie had suggested, things that disgusted him, but he guessed those questions had to be answered to get a full picture of where he rested on the kink scale and where his interests should take him.

By the time she came back from her phone calls, he was nearly done. She didn't interrupt him, or ask to see his answers, which he was grateful for. This was a little embarrassing, and he was well aware that she was in control for the moment which made him uncomfortable. But at the same time, he kind of liked it too. Hmmm.

"I've finished, do you want to go over the results with me?" He knew she'd want to know, whether he liked it or not, so he pushed down his need to dominate in every part of his life and called her over.

"Yes, please. If you don't mind." She pulled her chair nearer to his and sat down. When he nodded in agreement, she looked down at his phone screen. "92% voyeur, wow, that surprises me."

"Why?" He asked, feeling horrified that he'd done something that would make her think he was a weirdo.

"Because I thought you'd like to participate more, be more of an exhibitionist. It's not a bad thing, Lincoln, it just surprised me." She patted his arm and left her hand there. He liked that. "Let's see the rest."

Her lips moved slightly as she scrolled through, noting that he'd shown interest in rigging with raised eyebrows and a pursed grin, and nodded when she saw he was an experimentalist. "Okay, I see where we need to go. You're slightly more on the switch side than dominant, but I think that's the best of both worlds and I'm a switch too."

"Okay." He could only figure out what that meant through context, and he couldn't disagree. The thought of Roxie tying him up and teasing the fuck out of him was kind of…fucking hot. He wouldn't mind giving that a try at all.

"Non-monogamist?" She questioned and looked at him. "You sure about that? You don't seem like the type that would share easily."

"I'm not sure about that, but I've thought about group sex, at least. I don't know if I could totally get into it, but I like the idea in my head, at least." He answered her.

She scowled slightly, searched his face, then nodded. "It's an honest answer, at least."

"It is. I guess I'll just have to decide when and if the opportunity arises." He didn't really expect it would.

"Oh, I can arrange it if you'd like." She purred and winked at him with a sultry twist to her lips that nearly made his heart stop, it was so tempting.

He barely stopped his mouth from dropping open when she said that. "You could?"

"Of course, Lincoln. I'm a professional at this. It's not a game to me, you see? This is what I do in life. I seek gratification, whether it's sexual, my basic needs, or any other needs. But, if it can be a little kinky, as I'm fulfilling most of those needs, then it's always better."

She stared at him, her blue eyes dancing with amusement, but he knew it wasn't at his expense. She was just amused with the whole situation. That was fine, he would be too if the shoe were on the other foot. "I understand. So, um, the rest is all in red."

"Yeah, that's the more hardcore stuff that I don't go near." Her eyes darted away, and it made him wonder if she'd treaded into that world by mistake at some point. "It's not for me."

"That's fine. Obviously, it's not for me either."

"Yeah, I can see that." She finally looked at him and smiled softly. "So, we have an idea of where to begin, now we just need to decide when."

"Today?" He asked, trying not to sound too hopeful.

"We can start slow tonight, yes." She paused, thought for a moment, and then gave him a devilish grin. "After dinner. Do you think the results are accurate? Anything not on there you'd like to explore?"

"No, I think it pretty much has me pegged." He said it in total innocence but knew he'd said something when she snorted with glee in her eyes. "What did I say?"

"Pegged. That's a whole other kink, Lincoln." She laughed as she spoke and he couldn't help but smile with her. After a moment's thought, she seemed to change her mind about making him wait until after dinner. He wasn't about to complain about it. "You ready for your first lesson?"

"Well, thank fuck for that. I thought you were going to say we could start after I took another one of those tests." He laughed as he replied, relieved suddenly, but he wasn't sure why. "Where do we begin?"

4

Roxie

She led the way up the stairs to the room she'd reserved as his very own playroom. The door was always locked so she turned to him with her hand out. "Give me the key."

"Sure." He answered, and she could see how nervous he was as he fumbled in his pockets. "I've got it here somewhere."

He found the keyring that held the house keys and handed it to her. "Are you alright?" She asked.

He nodded and she unlocked the door and pushed it open. "Right, we haven't signed the contract yet, so I'm going to give you an overview of what can happen in here. Once the contract is signed, we'll begin the proper training."

She wasn't nervous or panicking about what would take place between the two of them here, it was a business relationship and that made the thought of sex with Lincoln, of being vulnerable to him, a thought she could handle. That contract removed emotions, even if a bond of some kind might form. There was a beginning and an end with that piece of paper. It might be something she'd have to remind him of later, that this wasn't a romantic relationship but a business one. The problem had cropped up with other protectors she'd had over the years, but not often.

Protectors, such an old-fashioned word for what would take place between them, but appropriate. Back in the day, protectors would provide for their mistresses, keep them housed, clothed, and fed. They were also supposed to take care of any offspring that cropped up from the arrangement, but Roxie knew that support likely hadn't happened in all cases. Which was another reason she took a pill every day, to avoid those messy entanglements.

He didn't have to pay for her housing unless he wanted to provide a place for her, but she didn't want to bring that up for now. Living apart from him would be a good thing. She'd be able to separate her personal space from his that way. Between maintaining her own place and having a contract, she'd stay on the straight and narrow.

"What's proper training?" He asked as she closed the door behind them.

She looked over at him and tried to judge how to word what came next. "Do you want a sub, Lincoln?"

"I don't want to degrade you and abuse you until you're black and blue, no." He shook his head, his brown hair moving in time with the movements. "But I would like to explore some bondage, the rope-tying stuff, and pushing the limits."

"Ah, now that's something that a lot of people get confused about. Pushing the limits can be bruises and welts. It can even be cuts and much worse, some people enjoy that, but I don't think you will." She narrowed her eyes and went to the bench that looked like a massage table. She pulled out wrist and ankle restraints from hidden compartments. "Tying someone up puts them in a very vulnerable position. They have to trust you, know that you won't go beyond their absolute hard no."

"Hard no? Hard limits?" He asked, looking at the restraints, not at her.

"Yes, the hard limits. Once you have me on here, I have to know that when I say stop, you'll push a little further for instance. This is about pushing limits, of course it is, but I might say stop in order to push you. That's why you have to know exactly where I draw the line and why I have to know that you'll comply with that line. Once I'm on this table, if I use that safe word and you ignore it, or you do something I've explicitly said not to, that's a breach of our contract. I'll leave and have no further contact with you."

"I understand." He nodded, swallowed hard, his face twisted in concern. "How will I know when you're testing me, pushing me?"

"You'll figure it out if you're observant. When I'm on the table you're the one in control, but we still have to read each other, listen to each other's breathing, look into each other's eyes." She moved close to him until he backed up against the wall. She splayed her fingers over his heart, her eyes on his. "We have to learn to know one another in a way that's not just hearts and butterflies, we have to know what a quickened heartbeat means."

She felt his heart pounding under her palm, saw the way his pulse skipped in his neck, and knew he was aroused. She didn't have to push her hips right up against his to know he was already hard and ready for her, because his lips were flushed as were his cheeks. She knew all these things were signs of his arousal, but would he know them in her? That's what he had to learn.

"When you can recognize what my body is telling you, I'll get on that table and let you tie me up, Lincoln," Roxie murmured the words, so he'd have to draw a little closer to hear her. His nostrils flared when he caught the scent of her perfume. Another sign of arousal. "I'll let you do whatever you want to me, within the limits of that contract. But only when you can recognize what my body wants."

She pulled away and smiled a triumphant smile when he made a sound of protest.

"Until then, I'll show you what this equipment is for, give you ideas on how to give and receive pleasure, and let you learn where you want to go exactly."

"I want you." He said plainly, his hands open in front of him. "I want to give you pleasure, be given pleasure by you, and explore all the areas you seem to know so well."

"I know them, yes, but I don't live in them, not like some." She didn't want to go into what she meant exactly, so she gave him a calming smile and tilted her head. "That's a choice you have to make, how deep you want to go. For now, let me show you some of the items in this drawer."

Lincoln listened carefully as she explained the use of nipple clamps and the variety of ways they could be used safely. "If you leave them on too long, they'll cause damage."

"These look interesting." He said, picking up what amounted to two bamboo sticks with rubber bands attached.

"They are very nice, when used properly." Her smile

was secretive but full of knowledge. "Even you might enjoy them."

"I might, I don't know." He shrugged and put the sticks down. "I don't know a lot about this kind of thing."

"You will soon enough. Now, these are for you." She opened another drawer full of cock rings, textured penis sleeves, vibrating prostate massagers, non-vibrating massagers, and masturbators. "And please don't be embarrassed. These are to enhance your pleasure, after all. And it's my job now to make sure you have just that."

"I see." He looked down at the items in the drawer.

Roxie hid a smirk when she saw him take a deep breath and frown down at the items laid out there.

"A prostate massager? That's really a thing?" He looked up at her with doubt dripping from his face.

"It is. Men that are brave enough to try them love them." She closed the drawer with a shrug and moved on. "These are restraints, silk ropes, handcuffs, and a few other things. I suggest, if you want to try rope-tying, that you practice on something else before you practice on me."

"Totally understand." Lincoln nodded in agreement and pointed at another drawer. "What's in there?"

"Lots of things." Roxie opened the larger drawer to reveal a rainbow of colors. Boxes of condoms, a first aid kit, sanitizer, wet wipes, and a lot more filled the drawer. "I know we've looked over some of this stuff before, when I first finished the room for you, but you need to become familiar with each item in this room."

"And the whips?" He pointed at a wall that held several styles, from riding crops to short whips with long handles, and longer whips too.

"Only if I agree on those, I'm afraid. You need to practice with them too if you want to use them. They're dangerous in untrained hands." Roxie pulled down a riding crop and held out her hand. "Give me your hand, palm up."

When he placed his hand in hers, she stroked the end of the crop against his palm.

"This flap of leather is soft, it feels nice, but when it hits your skin..." She flicked the crop just enough to get his attention without causing pain "...it can be either painful or stimulating. It's your job to figure out which is which."

"I see. This isn't as simple as I thought. From the sounds of it, there's a lot of danger involved." He looked around the room again, worry evident in the way his eyelids tightened up.

"Which is why there needs to be trust," she answered immediately. "You have to put effort into this if you want to get the most you can out of it. You can't just tie some rope around my tits and spank me with that plastic paddle and expect anything but boredom from me. You could damage my skin in very nasty ways if you aren't careful."

She watched him, waiting for him to work out whatever it was that had driven his thoughts inward, not on her. There was a lot to take in and a lot he'd need to do if he wanted to bring her into this room and do more than fuck her on the table. Was he prepared for that challenge?

"It's a little scary, but I suppose anything that involves ropes, whips, and restraints would be." He looked down at her, his eyes sure now.

He was the one that invaded her space now, backing her up until her hips bumped at the massage table. She looked up at him, her own excitement rising as she saw how intent his eyes were, how determined his mouth looked. "I want you screaming for my dick, Roxie. I want you begging me to fuck you. But most of all…"

Her breath caught in her chest as he spoke, as he drilled into her brain and probed around with eyes that could pierce steel. She was barely able to think as she waited for him to continue.

"I want to hear you whisper my name as you come apart around me." He almost whispered that last part, almost brought her to her knees.

It wasn't very often that a man could captivate her like that, not often at all, and Lincoln had done it with mere words. He might be more dangerous than she'd thought. Time to take control back, before this went further than she wanted it to.

"Then you'll have to work for it, won't you, Lincoln?" She crooked her left eyebrow and moved away from him, just enough to catch her breath while still facing him.

"I think I might, yes. You won't make this easy if I know anything about you." His gaze was still intense, burning into her soul, but she was able to smile without melting into a pool of fascinated goo at his feet.

"Well, good things don't come easy, do they?" She backed away from him again, further this time, until she stood in the doorway, peering in at him.

Did he realize she needed to get away from him before she broke her own rules? A quick glance showed a steady gaze with less heat burning from his eyes. Fuck, this was going to be hard, and it shouldn't be. She'd hated Lincoln when they were children, back in the good old days when her family lived minutes away from his.

Well, maybe hate was too strong. She couldn't stand to be around him because he'd always teased her, called her princess because that's how her parents had treated her: as if she were royalty. But that was another memory she didn't want to think about so she pulled her eyes away from his and put her hands on the doorframe. She wasn't sure if it was to keep her from running back into the room with him or to make sure she didn't allow herself to run away in undignified haste.

"I'll stay in here for a bit, I think." He said, waving his right arm around to indicate the room. "Do some studying."

The lilt of the remnants of his English accent was more pronounced, as if he knew how the sound drew women in. *Her* in, at that moment, she thought wryly. "That sounds like a plan. I'm going to check my phone, make a few calls."

"If you need anything, you know where I'll be. And would you like me to cook dinner?" His teasing smile, the one she was used to from him, was back in place and she decided he might do alright with this stuff, after all. He'd performed well last night, even without training, she reminded herself.

The thought renewed the flush on her skin and her need to run away, but she forced her feet to stay still. "Sure, that sounds nice. I'll come down when I get finished with my calls."

She'd call Wendy and Emily to let them know where she was for the moment, but that was an excuse more than anything. She also needed distance from Lincoln. It was too late to back out of the contract now, even if she really wanted to. She'd look like a coward if she put a stop to it all and that was one thing she had never been.

"Oh, by the way? I still hate you, contract or no."

With a wave of her hand, she left him finally and walked back to the living room.

"Of course, princess, I didn't expect that had changed at all." He chuckled behind her. Before, that mocking chuckle would have infuriated her, but now? Fuck, it made her body tingle in places it definitely shouldn't.

This was probably going to be one of the biggest mistakes of her life. She had far too many secrets, secrets that she would never tell Lincoln or anyone else. Secrets that she'd hide forever, no matter what it took. Somehow, she'd have to guard those secrets from Lincoln. And maybe try to enjoy what he had to offer her in the process. Maybe.

5

Lincoln

*L*incoln sat up against plush pillows, his duvet covered in papers, pens, and the tablet he used for personal matters. He had a laptop for personal use, but right now, the tablet sufficed. He had a document open on the tablet, inserting the items Roxie—still Chloe to him—had requested in the margins of the sample contract she'd printed for him.

He couldn't believe he was actually considering this. When she first said she wanted a contract he thought she was joking. Seems not, he mused as he picked up the final paper and went over her neat handwriting with narrowed eyes. He wanted to get this right, wanted to make this work, even if he thought it was silly.

Perhaps it wasn't so silly, though. He'd wondered

about the forceful way she said some things earlier. She would break the contract if he stepped over the line. Didn't that go against the whole dom/sub idea? He wasn't really looking to break her brain and make her a slavering slave, but he did want to learn to play with her, get down and dirty with her.

Which was just another sign that the old Chloe he used to know was gone. Memories of her dancing ballet again wanted to push that knowledge away, say it wasn't true, but it was. That innocent, sweet girl was gone. In the place of that frightened girl was an independent, capable woman who feared little.

Lincoln didn't want to think about the experiences she'd had that had made her into that new woman, not because he couldn't bear to know she'd been hurt but because he'd want to strangle whoever had crossed a line with her. Prison wasn't in his future, not if he could help it, so it was best not to think about men like her ex-boyfriend and let his team handle it. Tanya and the others could deal with the situation.

He glanced over to the nightstand when his phone started to buzz quietly.

"What's up, Tanya?" He asked, not surprised that his thoughts seemed to have conjured her up.

"Not much, there's no sign of the asshole that Roxie used to call a boyfriend near her place. I've not been able to track him down either." Tanya's voice purred into the phone, naturally sensual, even if she was doing her best to sound professional.

She was another capable woman in his life, as good at scheduling meetings without conflict as she was at security details.

"Alright. Have you heard from Kai?" Lincoln put down the tablet he still held in one hand. Kai Li was one of his best friends and had probably spent the day playing polo or, more likely in Myrtle Beach, golf. The man couldn't stay still which was why, despite being one of the richest men in the world, he was currently running the security detail that Tanya was a part of.

"Yeah, he's keeping tabs on the others tracking down the ex and those men after him. No sign that they're after Roxie, by the way, not from what I've seen so far."

"Good. Thanks for calling, Tanya. Is there anything else you need to tell me?" Lincoln asked, preparing to get back to the contract.

"That's all. I'll buzz you if there's anything new tonight." Tanya's voice held a wistful note that he knew she tried to suppress, so he ignored it. She could pine for him all she wanted to, she was too good an employee to fuck. Fucking her would make life messy and he didn't need more mess in his life right now.

"Alright, speak soon." He hung up before she could say anything else.

He went right back to tapping on his tablet, entering

an amount that was several times more than Roxie's previous salary as a payment amount. Once he'd read it over and decided everything she'd asked for was there, he emailed the contract to her. He didn't know if she'd still be up, she'd gone back to her hotel after he'd prepared dinner, but he hoped she would be.

He fell asleep waiting for a reply.

* * *

THE NEXT DAY Lincoln woke up to see she still hadn't responded. As much as he tried not to let it happen, a dark mood settled in and he spent most of the day growling at his phone to buzz already. Or ping. Or whatever noise it wanted to make to notify him that Roxie had responded. Shit.

He got up, dressed, and left the house to pace around on the sand, water surging up the beach to wet his feet. He should be enjoying the sunlight with a few beers and some good music while the soothing sound of the surf relaxed him but, oh no, Roxie was too busy to reply to him.

The hotel she was in had wi-fi, she'd told him that, and she had Internet on her phone, so why hadn't she responded? Was something…wrong?

Ice cold dread laced into his blood, shot down his spine as he started to wonder if someone or something was keeping her from replying to his email. *Or had she run away again?* Lincoln stopped dead on the hot sand, sunlight warming his suddenly icy skin, and looked back at the house, wondering if he should get his keys and drive over to the cheap room she'd rented.

He could just picture how she'd glare at him if he did show up there and everything was fine. Her shoulders would draw back, her lovely face pulled down in a frown, hands on her hips. A smile replaced the worry on his face, but it didn't stop him from glancing at his phone again, in case he'd missed a notification.

He'd call Kai or Tanya and ask them to do a stealthy check on her, but what if she tried to call and he missed it?

Lincoln kicked a lump of sand and headed back into the house. He'd wait one more hour, then he'd go over there. With a calm he didn't feel, he showered and shaved, and put on clean clothes. He wasn't the kind to panic, even when the situation excused it. Logic ruled his mind on most occasions. The exception to that rule was Chloe, who now insisted on being called Roxie.

Still, panic wouldn't help the situation, so he decided to just send Tanya a message and have her drive by and do a quiet recon. His brows knitted together in frustration when he got her response.

Sorry, Lincoln, I can't today. I'm with my daughter at the movies. I could drive by after?

That wasn't very helpful, but Tanya had a six-year-old daughter named Myra who needed her mom's attention. Lincoln knew that—he'd met the girl on several occasions and liked her intelligent, inquisitive eyes.

If you don't hear from me by the time the movie is finished, I'd appreciate that. Otherwise, I'll text you if I hear anything.

Tanya didn't bother to respond but he saw the 'seen' notification that showed up on the messenger. That's all he needed to know to get on with his day. Now, if only Roxie would do the same thing.

Brushing his right hand through his hair, Lincoln answered a few emails from work and a message from his sister. She was a fertility doctor in New York, with a title that went on for a mile. Normally, June was so busy he didn't hear from her for months, but she was attending some gala or other and wanted to know if Lincoln would be there. It would be a good time for them to meet up, since they so rarely saw each other now.

Lincoln allowed his sister to distract him for a while but when he heard a car engine pulling up outside his house, he knew it had to be the woman he needed distracting from. The only other person but him who knew the code to the security gate out front was Roxie. Wincing at the way his heart thudded a little harder in excitement, he'd never been a sappy guy so being excited to see her brought him down a notch or two, he went to the front door to wait on her.

His first impulse was to yell at her, demand to know why she hadn't answered his messages immediately, while checking her over for injuries or other harm. Instead, he stood in the doorway, one hand on the door, the other in his pocket with a bland smile in place. Okay, so he was going loopy over her for some reason, he could deal with it on his own. She didn't need to know anything about it.

"Hi." She said when she made it to the door, a faint smile on her lips as if it was only the lingering remains of a smile and not meant for him. She looked up at him with a frown knitting her eyebrows together, before she looked down at the ground. "I had to do some thinking, so before you blast me and ask why I didn't answer your messages, that's why."

"And what did you decide, princess?" Lincoln winced again, not sure why that word had slipped out. He only ever called her princess to annoy her, but that's not what he wanted to do. Now, she'd bristle up in anger and blast him with some profanity-laden directive stating where and how far he could shove it.

He watched her and saw that her smile stretched a little wider. Perhaps she'd let the dig go then.

"I decided that I'd come and see you. It's not the best time to be in my life, but then I doubt there's ever really a good time. So long as we can both stay grounded, know that this is only about learning and having some fun, then I can go on with the contract." She looked up finally, tension around the skin of her eyes and in the shadows that turned the light blue orbs into a cloudy grayish-blue.

He knew she was worried when she left the last time, so this wasn't that much of a surprise. "I've had affairs before, Roxie. I have a life that leads me all over the world. I don't have a lot of time for becoming wrapped up in a long relationship. I don't think you have a lot to worry about."

"That's good to know." She hitched the bag over her shoulder a little higher and tilted her head. "Can I come in?"

"Sure, sorry. I didn't mean to leave you on my doorstep like that," Lincoln answered, stepping out of the way to let her into his home.

"Shall we sign the papers and begin then? There's a few hours left in the day, after all." She gave him a coy smile over her shoulder as she walked into his living room.

"There are a few, yes." He said, checking the watch on his wrist to see that there were quite a few hours left. His blood pulsed in his veins, straight down to his groin, as he thought about what she might be able to teach him in those few hours.

"Good, I thought we'd start by practicing on you, so you know what kind of sensations come from some of those toys you have upstairs." Her smile this time was seductive, luring him into her gaze.

"Oh?" He managed to get out through a throat that had suddenly gone…tight. Even as a teenager she'd been, somehow, innocently seductive. Now that she was grown and knew how to make a man pay attention to her and only her, well, she nearly made him forget his own name.

"Yes, just sign these, Lincoln and we can get started." She pulled the papers out of the bag she'd put down on the floor when she took a seat on the couch. There were two copies of the contract, one for each of them. He swiftly took the pen she handed him to sign on the line where his name had been typed on both pages.

After she signed her own name Roxie put one set of papers in her bag and left the other set out for him. "Ready?"

He didn't give two fucks about the papers at the moment, he just wanted her. He looked over the short black skirt she had on, topped with a slouchy black t-shirt, and couldn't help but wonder what hid underneath them.

Her breasts were much larger than they'd been all those years ago, implants that had become supple over the years. They were still nice to hold in his hands, but that wasn't what had him intrigued. Did she have on a silky black lace bra that matched her panties or did she have on nothing at all under her clothes? If he was lucky, he'd soon find out.

"I'm ready, yes." He shook himself out of his daze and followed her up the stairs.

6

Lincoln

"Get up on the table, please." Roxie directed him as they walked into his playroom, making Lincoln pause in the doorway.

"How do I know you aren't going to tie me down and do terrible things to me?" He asked, only half-joking.

This wasn't Chloe anymore, a thought he kept thinking, even now. This was a woman who was still a mystery to him and while he didn't really think she'd do anything to harm him, she might hurt him to make a point.

"Oh, but I plan to do the most horrible..." Roxie paused, came close to him, her head tilted up to look right into his eyes, and grinned with pure satisfaction "...Terrible, awful things to you, Lincoln. Things that will make your knees shake as your brain explodes. But you'll beg for more."

He gulped, glanced down at her knees, down to the shiny black stilettos she wore, before going back up to her head. "But you're not going to leave me there, are you? You will let me go?"

"That's where trust comes in, Lincoln. Either you trust me and make this first step, or you don't, and we call it quits. So, which will it be?" The quirk of her left eyebrow emphasized the dare in her eyes.

"I have one question." He replied, his fears gone now that he understood this was a test to see how much he trusted her. She was a virtual stranger, but he knew, deep down the girl he used to know was still in there. He hoped.

"And what's that?" She moved away from him a little and crossed her arms under her breasts. The soft push of her breasts against the fabric of her shirt almost distracted him, but he held on.

"Do you want me naked or no?" It was Lincoln's turn for smugness as her face twisted into a perplexed look.

"Oh, right. Well, down to your briefs, at least." She finally said, when it dawned on her why she might want him naked. "Or boxers, as it may be."

"I see," Lincoln grumbled low and deep. She might know how to use every part of her anatomy and her voice to seduce, but he wasn't a stranger to seducing women either. The smug look came back as he undressed, he couldn't help it. He might be the one that was about to get up on a table and dance to her tune, but he knew he could pull her in to wanting him.

"Good. Now, up here." Roxie patted the black leather that covered the table and waited for his compliance. When he was sprawled on the table she moved up to his right side, his head facing the door, his feet facing the wall, and took his right wrist in her hand. "Ready?"

"I am, yes." He answered, not afraid but definitely turned on. He didn't know exactly what she had in mind, but he suspected it would be good, no matter what.

"Now, if you start to feel any anxiety at all, I want you to use the safe word, okay?" Her voice was business-like, efficient even as she moved around, closing the cuffs around his wrists before she moved down to his feet.

"Blue waffles, I got it." He repeated their safe word, something she'd snickered about so much he'd eventually looked it up. He didn't recommend anyone else to do the same, but as a safe word, it worked. The image immediately cooled down his libido when her cool hands touched his feet. "Go for it, Roxie."

"Thank you, Lincoln." She smiled at him as she latched the first cuff together. Maybe it should have surprised him that he didn't feel any anxiety at all, but he didn't. That was down to how professional she'd been so far, he decided, as she moved to his other foot.

He watched her latch the last cuff around his ankle and took a deep breath. "What am I supposed to do now?"

"Well, you need to pay attention to what your body tells you, how you respond to everything from the lights going dim..." She paused to do just that, adjusting the light until the room was not dark, but romantically lit by the recessed lighting "...To the sound of the drawer opening. These are all things that will be signals to your sub, or to you if you choose to carry on in that position, of what will arouse them or cool their passion."

She moved to his left, to the drawers she'd filled with a rainbow of toys. "Can you hear the way it sounds when I open this drawer?"

"Yes," he answered immediately, but wondered why she'd asked him that.

"Now, pay attention." She opened another drawer, but this time he noticed a slight difference in the sound. This drawer held different items, but he didn't know which yet. "Listen to them closely."

Each drawer sounded a little different, and he could start to see her point. The sound of each drawer closing caused a little disappointment, but she soon opened another and he was surprised to find himself...curious.

"Now, we'll begin." She moved to face him, a scrap of

cloth in her hand, her top gone to reveal a black lacy number that held up her breasts and disappeared below the skirt. "This is silk."

She moved the scrap over his face, down his shoulders, and across his chest. "Seduction, play with your sub isn't just about pinching nipples and whippings. It's about bringing satisfaction and sometimes that can be done with a soothing touch. The whisper of cloth over their skin."

Lincoln's eyes closed when she began to touch him with the silk, imagining it as her fingers or her lips, until she started to speak. That was when he focused on what she was saying, despite how hard it was to bring his attention back to reality. Her voice was pitched low, a seductive tone but not too low to hear. She was teaching him, even if it was hard to concentrate.

"Okay, but what if that touch causes more...arousal than comfort or soothing?" He asked, not sure if he should speak now, but willing to take whatever punishment she might want to dole out to him.

"That's kind of the point, but..." She paused, thought for a moment, and gave a half-smile before she responded "...If that causes more problems, then you'll have to learn to soothe your sub in different ways. That's your job."

"My job? Isn't the idea to do as I please when I'm the

dominant one?" He frowned as he asked the question, still confused about all of this.

"Pay attention, Lincoln." She spoke louder suddenly, her body ramrod straight. "This is a partnership. Unless that's specifically stated in the contract, your job is to dominate your sub, yes, but it's to do it in a way that satisfies your sub's needs."

"And that doesn't always mean being an asshole to them 24/7?" He grinned, but the grin faded when she moved up by his head, her lips close to his but out of reach.

"Say that again and I'll strap your head down, too." Her fingers moved into his hair and tugged lightly, enough to let him know she could pull much harder if she wanted to. "But, if it's in a future contract, so be it."

"I see. It's not in ours, so no." He watched her, excited at the control she'd taken, but also wondering what it would be like to have *her* on this table. He was starting to get the point of tonight's lesson now. She was running him through the basics of it all.

A pleased smile eased the frown she'd worn and her hand came down to his chest to stroke one of his nipples. Lincoln inhaled sharply when the touch proved pleasurable, far more exciting than it had ever felt when anyone else touched him there. "You understand now. Good."

Ah, the touch was a reward then, for answering correctly. Nice.

For a moment, Lincoln wished he'd worn something looser than the boxer briefs he had on, maybe baggier boxer shorts would have hidden just how nice his reward had been.

Moments passed while Roxie dug around in the drawers, rifling through objects, picking some up before putting them down. Lincoln couldn't tell what each one was yet, but tied down to the table, he began to understand what being a submissive entailed. There was no escape, no way to demand to have your needs met, you could only wait and see what the person in charge did to, or for, you. And certainly no way to hide the effect that Roxie had on him, either.

"This will work for now," Roxie said with a note of satisfaction.

Lincoln's eyes closed, worried that she was about to do something to him that would leave him embarrassed. But wasn't that what he was paying her to do? Teach him about all of this? Being strapped down was a brilliant idea on her part, he now had an inkling of what she would feel like once the roles were reversed. He wondered how she'd deal with that.

"Open your eyes, Link, you can't hide from me here, no matter how hard you try." She said the words softly, hypnotically, to draw his eyes open.

"What are those for?" He asked, staring at something that had pads connected to wires that were connected to some kind of machine.

"It's a tens machine, it's for muscle therapy when in the hands of most people, but in my hands, yours at some later date, it can cause an intense sensation in the breasts and nipples. I want you to know how it works, should you decide to use it on a sub." Her left eyebrow was arched again, a smile in place that simultaneously made him as hard as a rock, but also chilled him to the bones.

The cold part came from the fact that she looked as if she knew exactly how much control she was now in, the hard came from being eager to know what kind of pleasure she had in store for him.

"You see, Link." He winced as she again used the pet name he hated so much. She did that on purpose, he knew it. "Pleasure doesn't have to come from a hand, or a mouth, or even skin in general. It can come from many sources. You just have to know how to use them and use them wisely."

She pulled plastic tabs off each pad and placed two cold, sticky globs to each side of his left nipple and two around his right. He had an inkling what the machine would do, electrical stimulation of his nerves that could prove very pleasurable, or very...painful. In the wrong hands.

"Roxie." He started to protest, but she gently placed a hand on his forehead, stopping the flow of words.

"Trust me, Lincoln, you have to trust me." Her words soothed the sudden burst of fear that made him tense up.

Their eyes met and Lincoln felt his body begin to relax. This wouldn't be so bad. He had to trust her. Experience the moment and trust her. Just as she'd have to trust him when she was in this same position.

He felt blood throb through his cock as he imagined her lying here in his place. That's when Roxie turned the machine on, and he felt the first whispers of sensation around his nipples. "Fuck!"

"Nice, isn't it?" Roxie purred with a smug smile. She knew exactly what she was causing and enjoyed every moment of power she had over him.

Lincoln's body and brain responded to that in a way he hadn't expected. He loved seeing her in so much control, even though he now wanted his own turn at it. Seeing the woman that he now called Roxie so in control of the moment was intoxicating. She was beautiful, powerful, and every moment with her enthralled him.

"Now." She continued when he didn't respond. "I'll turn it up a little at a time."

But instead of turning up the dial, she put the small, handheld device down and placed her hands on his chest, just below his nipples. He wanted to ask her what she was about to do but stopped himself. She looked so good when she was in control, he didn't want it to stop.

But then, wasn't the whole idea here that he was supposed to challenge her to be a good dom? Make her give him what he wanted, even when she was the one in control? He was certain he'd read that in some of his studying. Maybe that was more about brats, though? It didn't matter, not when her hands were skimming the top of his boxer briefs in a very suggestive way.

A way that suggested she'd go further if he just gave the right response. But what was the right response? To beg her to touch him? To put her hand down his shorts and stroke him?

He groaned in frustration, knowing that if he did the wrong thing she'd back off.

"What's wrong, Link?" She teased, her finger sliding over the very tip of his hard cock now. She'd avoided it until he groaned, now she ran her finger very deliberately down into his shorts just enough to slide down the tip a little more. "You have to tell me what you want."

"I want you to touch me." The words burst from between his lips before he could stop them.

"How do you want me to touch you, Lincoln?"

He could barely think as that finger of hers slid down again, deeper to slide along the length of him. She paused, her breasts nearly touching him, her lips so close to his that he could almost feel them.

"Where do you want me to touch you, Lincoln?" He felt the brush of her lips and thought his brain would explode. But he hadn't been paying attention to her other hand and he paid for it when he felt the fluttering, electric sensation from the electrodes increase.

The sensation made him gasp in delighted surprise, left his brain adrift as the hand down his shorts splayed out before it grasped around his girth.

"Is this what you want, Link?" She asked with delicious sternness. "You have to answer me, you know? Otherwise, I'll just stop."

She pulled her hand away and stood up straight, her face as stern as her voice. He wanted to please her, wanted to do this right, but he didn't know what the right answer was!

"I don't." He started, but his throat was dry, closed off as he tried to speak. He swallowed, looked over her tempting body, and tried again. "I want whatever you want, Roxie."

"Very good answer, Lincoln." Her smile was pleased this time. "You deserve a reward."

He was confused when she pushed a button and the table lowered down to the floor. "This is the part where you show me how well you can use your mouth, Lincoln. Show me how good you are now."

She knelt above his shoulders, her hands on each side of his waist, and lowered the sweet flesh of her pussy down to his mouth. And turned the dial up on the electrodes just as she did so. Fuck, she was going to kill him.

But at least he knew now that she didn't have any underwear on at all. Only a lace top that he really wished she'd take off.

7

Roxie

She shouldn't have done this, but the longer she'd looked at him strapped down on that table, the more she'd wanted to ride his cock. The need to fuck him overwhelmed her unexpectedly, so this was the next best thing. It would teach him more about what it was like to give pleasure while not being able to control his own, she told herself as his tongue lashed at her folds.

He found the right spot quickly and she had to adjust her position, sit up a little higher, when all she wanted was to bend further down and deep throat his gorgeous cock. She wanted to groan his name, beg him for more, trade him places, but she had to teach him how to do this right. The only way he'd know what to do was to experience the other side of it. That's what she'd told herself when she came up with this bright idea anyway, she thought, furiously trying to distract herself from the need to let go and explode as quickly as she could. He was talented with his tongue, but she had to be in control.

When his hips twitched on the table, she moved just enough to push his shorts down. His lips were sealed around her clit, promised her mere seconds until she rocketed into space, but maybe if she distracted herself from his lips...

She pulled her body away from his face to swallow down what she could of him without warning. She hadn't even gripped his cock to guide him into her throat, just took him in, and her reward was the jerk of his hips as he groaned in total abandon. Perhaps even submission, she couldn't help but think smugly.

What guy was truly in control, for real, when his dick was in someone's mouth? Roxie hummed in delighted happiness, eager to take back control. She hadn't been sure how Lincoln would react to being strapped down like this, but he'd proven himself a willing learner.

Having him in her mouth was almost as good as having his mouth on her. She enjoyed the taste of him on her tongue, the way he felt, the sensual way his hips moved against her face. Here his scent, his real scent permeated the air, making her inhale him deeply, both in her mouth physically, and through her nose. This was the Lincoln most people would never know, and the one she couldn't help but want to know more about.

No matter how much she might deny that to herself.

When his breathing changed, when he started to make small noises in his throat, when his hips thrust faster, she saw those things for what they were - signals. She pulled herself up, got off the table, despite his groan of protest, and pushed a button to bring the table back up to its resting height. She was denying herself and him, but he'd learn a lesson from that too.

"The time we spend in here is meant for exploring a world of pleasure, and with that comes learning pleasure in denial." She spoke softly, watching his face when his eyes met hers.

His eyebrows pulled together, and his lips flattened out. "Pleasure in denial? I'm about to bust, how can I find pleasure in that?"

"In putting it off, of course. 'Edging' some call it." She hit another button and the table began to move so that Lincoln's feet were now on the floor, his head just above hers. She poked at another button and she saw his eyes go wide. The electric stimulation had just gone up a notch. "Is it painful?"

"No, it's strange, good, but not painful." He shook his head and she moved closer to inspect his riveting brown eyes. They were almost yellow now, more amber than chocolate.

"Good." She ran her left hand down his face, along his neck, and danced her fingers down his chest before she moved away again. "I've denied us both a chance to finish because it reminds me I need to be in control when I'm the one standing here. And it teaches you to wait. To be patient. To take what you're given and accept it."

"But..." He started but she immediately put a finger over his mouth.

"No buts, Link. Those are the rules. They'll be the same rules you'll impose when it's my turn to be on that table." She could see the effect those words had on him and smiled. His eyes closed and a faint smile traced over his features. "Exactly. You're picturing me there now, and that is something else you must learn. Everything you say or do can be a directive, a touch, a present even."

"Or it can be torture," Lincoln answered, his eyes open and on hers again.

"Exactly. You're learning fast." She cupped his testicles with her left hand, gently fondling the globes when he moaned in appreciation. "You'll learn a lot about me, but even more about yourself, as the weeks pass, Lincoln. Then you'll be ready to decide which side of this table you really want to be on."

"But you seem to enjoy being on that side so much,

Roxie. Are you sure you won't influence me to stay on this side of it?" He asked, a dare in his eyes.

"Only you can decide, Lincoln. And believe me, if you aren't meant to be on this side, you'll know it and so will I. You won't be satisfied with how you perform, and I will be sorely disappointed and unfulfilled. It's not rocket science, really. Or, you might just be a switch like me. That's nothing to be ashamed of."

"No, I suppose not." His head fell back against the table, his arms hanging from the wrists still trapped in the clasps. "Are we done or is there more tonight?"

"I think..." She paused, studying him, wondering just how far she could take him "...I think you deserve to have some enjoyment out of the night, at least."

"Thank fuck." She heard him whisper as she sank to her knees in front of him. She suspected he thought he'd said it low enough she wouldn't hear, but she had.

Instead of making her reconsider her gift, she knew it was the right thing to do. He was on the edge of frustration, it wouldn't take her long to wring the final moments out of him. And then she'd be able to get back to her own life for the rest of the evening.

His cock, hard, long, and florid with life seemed to wave in the air, directing her to where he needed to be touched the most. She smiled as she took it in her hand and licked the tip slowly. A quick glance up showed he was watching her, eager to see her lips around his cock.

"You do realize you're still tied to this table, right? I could get up and leave you here for a while if I wanted to." She stroked him with her hand as she spoke, her eyes locked to his.

That look of worry came back, but now it gave way to a new excitement, something she wasn't sure she'd see. Thrill at the slightest hint of danger. Not real danger, but danger that the adventure would be over, was something new for him. It seemed he was enjoying being on that side of the table. She'd have to think about it more later. Figure out what to do with him next time she brought him in here.

"Or I can stay right here and jerk you off until you come all over my face and chest. Would you like that, Lincoln?" The words were spoken on the back of a moan, her body twinging in need as she saw how red his face was now, how hot and swollen his lips were with his need. Every inch of him screamed desire, need, but she had to hold back, had to give him what he needed, not what she needed.

"I'd like that, Roxie, yes. I never thought I would, but yes, I want to come all over your pretty face, and over those gorgeous breasts of yours. Please, may I?"

Oh, now that almost broke her will. He'd finally caught on. He'd finally asked for permission to do something. "You may, when you're ready, Lincoln."

Relief escaped his throat as a sigh, as the falling of his

head back against the table again. But his head soon lifted to look down at her, his mouth open as he watched her hand move, then shifted his gaze to her eyes. "Come for me, Lincoln. Come all over me."

"Fuck." He gasped just as his cock twitched in her hand, his hips motionless at last.

She heard him groan deeply just as the first pulse of his satisfaction hit her on the chin, then further down. The drop slid down her left breast just as she used her thumb to squeeze him a little harder, make him groan a little more. Men were so easy.

She hid a chuckle and continued to stroke him until he slumped against the table, his eyes bleary but satisfied. "All done?"

"I think that was a little too soon, wasn't it?" He rolled his eyes at himself. "Sorry. I think I got too caught up in the moment."

"No, you did exactly what I wanted you to do actually." She said as she got to her feet, turned off the tens machine, and pulled away the electrodes. "I wanted you to come then and made you do it."

She spoke as nonchalantly as she would if she were telling him she'd ordered a new shirt for him or made him dinner. There was no need to be cruel at all. This was a lesson. "You'd had enough for one night, you needed relief, tonight was not the night to deny you. Maybe next week."

"Wait." He said as she began to undo the clasps around his wrists, then his ankles. "You don't plan to be on the table next week?"

"If I think you're ready, yes. If not, then no." She stood back as he pulled up his boxer briefs and frowned at her.

"I want you on this table." He turned her to the table and came up to stand close to her. "I want you just like this, Roxie."

"Then you have to show me that you can do it, Link. You have to prove you can do it right." She wasn't sure what had gotten into her. She'd only just told him he wasn't ready, but here she was, daring him to do it now. Was this her sub side, her bratty side, wanting him to prove to them both that he could be the alpha not just in the office, but here in his playroom too?

Maybe it was, she thought, and decided to play it out. To see how far he could go.

"I can do it, right, Roxie. It's not like I'm a complete virgin, you know." He took her right hand in his, slid it up the table as his eyes held her in place against the black leather. Fuck, her nipples ached for his touch so much that even the heat of his chest made them hard.

She waited, breath held as her hand slid through the cuff, as he clasped the closure and let his own hand come back down. "I think you want this more than you're daring to let on, Roxie, and making excuses to us both why you should be the one in control."

"I..." She started, but let the words go when her other hand was suddenly caught in a cuff. The atmosphere, her brain, her needs changed and she was his suddenly. All his.

"We don't need this." She heard him say as he sank to the floor and pulled the skirt from her hips. He nudged at an ankle and she lifted her foot so that he could pull the skirt away. At the same time, she felt the cuff close around it, then the other ankle. Fuck.

She was caught now, but if the promise in his eyes meant anything, she wasn't going to be too upset about that.

"Now, let me see." He moved away to the drawers and began to open them. She already knew what each drawer sounded like and her breath caught when he found the drawer that held nipple clamps and devices that would torture her clit. But in a devilishly delicious way.

"Let's put the table down first, shall we?" He moved back to put the table on all four legs before he produced the devices she loved to dread.

He held two purple nipple suckers and he seemed to know exactly what they were for. He licked the one in his right hand and adjusted it until she hissed. Her eyes met his again and she saw him nod in a satisfied, but questioning way.

"That's good." She answered, her heart racing as he brought the other one up to her firm breast.

"These are gorgeous, you know?" He asked as he hefted the weight of the right one. "But all of you is beautiful, Roxie."

He stroked the bottom of her breast gently before he pushed the button that turned the tiny vibrator in each sucker on.

"Fuck."

"That good?" He asked, an eyebrow crooked in question. He wasn't smiling now, his look was pure curiosity instead.

"It is." Roxie managed to get out just before she gave in to the sensation coursing through her breast.

"Let's try the other one then." He murmured and she wanted to shout at him to stop, but he was taking the reins in his own hands. She couldn't back down now.

The breath of a moan that she let out was all she could manage as the pleasure intensified to double what it had been before. Both her nipples were suctioned and vibrating now. If she stayed there long enough the sensation alone might get her off, but she saw Lincoln turn back to the drawer and lift another sucker out. This one was for somewhere totally different.

"I don't know a lot about these kinds of toys, Roxie, I

have to be honest, but I can guess what most are for. Let's try this one, shall we? See what kind of reaction I get from it." He spoke softly again, driving her mad with the timbre of his voice. He made it all even worse when he slid a finger between her legs, down into her folds, to find her more than ready for his touch. "Ah, very good. Still wet from my kisses."

That wasn't all but she decided not to speak. If he wanted to take the reins, he'd have to work words out of her. She set her mouth in a defiant purse and glared up at the ceiling. Which was hard to do when your nipples were vibrating happily and your clit was being teased by a very knowledgeable finger.

"I don't think you need the toy at all, do you, Roxie? You're already so turned on you can't stand it." He leaned down to purr this in her ear and she nearly screamed with the need to come. Even her hips twisted up in time with his finger. Until he slid that finger down, joined it with another, and slid both inside her.

She groaned as her head fell back and her body tensed. It was too much, but not enough, and when his palm ground into her clit in just the right way, it was lights out. She couldn't help but moan his name as the world blew apart and she sucked in air, trying to hold on for dear life to her soul, but her hands were clasped in the cuffs and she couldn't get out of them.

"Fuck." The word spit out of her mouth when she felt his hair against her leg and felt his tongue on her clit.

"You taste like candy."

She didn't give a fuck what she tasted like, so long as he didn't stop tasting her. She thought it would become too much, that she'd push his head away and beg him to stop torturing her poor body. That didn't happen. What happened was her hips left the table, her skull dug into the leather, and her soul flung itself out joyfully without even a look back as he got her off again with a tight suck on her clit.

She was in so much trouble, the thought thumped in her brain as the world came back into focus and she looked down at a very pleased Lincoln. He had fucked her world up and he hadn't even fucked her tonight. He'd taken the lead now, though, and that was what he was paying for. To teach him to do what he'd just done, only to someone else. Why did that knowledge cause a pain in her chest?

8

———————

Roxie

"What's this charity event for?" Kitty asked as Roxie pulled into a parking space at the resort Dylan James now owned.

He was going to have a bigger empire than the Thompsons if he kept it up at this rate, Roxie thought to herself before she opened the door and got out. "It's for a new shelter, but I think this one might be out in California or somewhere. You remember those really bad fires out there last year? A lot of people lost their homes and some woman out there has a mansion going moldy, so she's decided to turn it into a place for those in need following natural disasters."

"Oh, sounds like a good cause then." Kitty got out,

grabbed her bag, and closed her door while she spoke. "Thanks for inviting me to perform tonight. I appreciate the chance."

"You're ready so it's my pleasure." Roxie took Kitty's elbow as they headed for an elevator. "Let's find Emily and we'll get you set up."

"Why didn't Lincoln come with you again?" Kitty asked and Roxie shrugged.

"He's not my boyfriend or anything, you know? He said he was coming but he'd be here later than I needed to be so, yeah, he's coming anyway." Roxie hadn't exactly told Kitty about her arrangement with Lincoln, or anybody else for that matter, but Kitty was observant and caught on to how often Lincoln texted her when they were apart.

An hour passed while Roxie followed Emily around the poolside bar and the stage set up in front of the pool. Emily was nervous, but she always was at these things.

"How's it going with you and Lincoln?" Emily asked blithely as if she hadn't just picked up a glass with a death-grip that should have shattered the delicate vessel.

"It's fine," Roxie answered, looking at Emily closely. "Why?"

"I was just curious. I know he's very intrigued by you." Emily flitted away to take up a position at the back of the bar and nodded. "We'll be able to see Kitty fine from back here."

Roxie let Emily's curiosity go, knowing if she didn't answer something else would grab her attention. Emily wasn't an airhead or dim, by any stretch of the imagination, she was just overworked from having her irons in too many fires at once. She had a family of her own to take care of, a husband, and life with them. Mixing all these charity events into it just made the poor woman overworked, even if she was still beautiful while she did it all.

"Great, I'm going to go check on Kitty, okay? The guests are starting to arrive, and I want to make sure she's not freaking out back there." Roxie swung around, enjoying the swing of the black poplin floral Oscar De La Renta dress she'd borrowed from Wendy. It was a classy dress and perfectly suited to a warm evening outside.

Only, she didn't get to giggle as she was about to because the giggle died in her throat. Lincoln had just walked out to the pool area with a very famous woman on his arm. A woman that Roxie recognized because she was in a very popular television series about sex and magical dragons. Naomi Thorne made hot sex even hotter, and there was a popular saying that Naomi was so hot that fire couldn't burn her, but her sexy co-stars might with those sex scenes.

The woman had been a model before she became an actress and as Roxie faced her in real life, she could see why the woman had been a model. She really was beautiful, even with a bare minimum of makeup. Roxie frowned, looking down at her borrowed dress and compared it to the red silk sheath that encased Naomi's body. The red dress enhanced every single one of Naomi's curves and somehow made Roxie look childish in her stylish, tasteful, but not very sexy poplin dress.

Roxie felt anxious as she watched Lincoln take Naomi around and introduce her. She shouldn't be worrying about who Lincoln showed up with, and why he hadn't told her he was bringing a date. Instead, she should be focusing on Kitty. This gig could really be a break for the other woman. She could start doing shows and events on her own if she performed well tonight. That's what was making her anxious, Roxie decided as she finally dragged her eyes away from Lincoln and the beautiful, very blonde Naomi.

Tonight could mean Kitty got out of the Pussy Shack, a place they all hated because of the name, plus the million other reasons. Yeah, Kitty had the other job as an instructor, but Roxie knew she didn't want to do that for the rest of her life. She wanted to provide a good life for her kids and hold her head up high. Tonight's performance could be the start of that for Kitty.

Roxie couldn't stop herself from looking around for Lincoln one last time with a glare. Oh shit, he was headed towards her, Roxie saw with wide-eyed horror.

Fuck, run away, run away raced through her brain but her feet wouldn't move. Which was unfortunate because beautiful Naomi Thorne might be, but agile she was not.

Naomi managed to trip over thin air, spilled the glass of champagne she was sipping all over the borrowed dress Roxie wore, and stared at Roxie in horror. "I'm so sorry!"

"Lincoln Christopher Young!" Roxie shouted, furious at him for some reason. Okay, if she was going to be furious it should be with the woman that had just spilled her drink over her, but instead, her brain decided to focus on Link. "How could you?"

Emily, who'd been behind Naomi, rushed up to Roxie just as Naomi's hands reached out for Roxie's dress. Both women were fluttering around her like birds trying to wipe away the liquid, but Roxie only had eyes for Lincoln. Fuck, was he really that stupid? The confused look on his face said he was—it seemed he had no idea why she was staring at him with daggers in her eyes.

"Just, oh don't worry about it, I have to change to perform later anyway." Roxie walked away from the trio but Emily followed.

"How is it you know Lincoln's middle name? Did you make that up? I don't think anybody knows his middle name, not even Google."

"I saw it on a form at work," Roxie replied, hoping

that was plausible. "I think."

"Okay. I'll let you get organized and see you later, okay?"

"Fine, honey, enjoy the show." Roxie kissed Emily's cheek and went into the changing area where Kitty was applying makeup and getting into her costume. She had a long, virginal-looking white nightgown over a pair of white leather booty shorts and a white leather corset. She looked amazing and Roxie told her that as she walked in.

"Thanks. How is it outside?" Kitty asked, not looking away from the lit mirror she sat in front of.

"Fine. Full of assholes as usual, but fine." Roxie replied, although there was only one real asshole that she'd seen. Lincoln.

Why had he brought another woman to the event? How could he do that to her?

Why did it matter to her? She thought snidely to herself. He's just a client, remember? Nothing more. So what if he's going to show off the things she'd taught him over the last week to the gorgeous actress? So what if he did take that woman to the playroom that Roxie worked so hard on? And who the fuck cared if that actress got to enjoy some of those toys they hadn't played with yet before she did? There was no exclusivity clause in their contract, and Lincoln had never made any promises. Only that he'd always wear protection and check regularly for STDs. That was it.

"What's up, Rox? You look pissed."

"Nothing," Roxie replied shortly, but then sighed and turned around. "Sorry, it's not your fault. I just don't feel like this all of a sudden."

"Which is when you usually perform best, I have to say." Kitty quipped but her face was serious. "Being upset comes out on the stage with you as magic."

"I hope you're right." Roxie pulled off the damp dress, revealing a dark purple bustier and a flirty wisp of purple silk that covered the purple panties she wore. "At least I don't have to change."

"I wish I'd worn something I could wear under my clothes, but these shorts are just too hot to wear off-stage, and I just got them for this show." Kitty shrugged again and put the last of her eyeliner away. "Chair's all yours. I'm going to check with the DJ that he has our music."

"Good idea. I'll be out in a bit." Roxie sighed deeply as her friend left the room. She had an hour to kill before Kitty left the stage. Time to check her makeup, curl her hair, and get ready to spend the evening smiling at people she didn't know.

When she heard the DJ say Kitty's name, Roxie

wandered out to stand in the wings of the stage. She spotted Lincoln with Emily and Dylan right away, the actress by his side. Roxie frowned but didn't move. If this was the kind of student Lincoln was, then he sucked. Imagine bringing another woman to watch her perform on stage.

Holy fucking moly, what a fucking idiot he was. How ungrateful was he to do something like that?

She didn't want to admit that what was really eating her up was the idea of Lincoln fucking anybody that wasn't her. She had feelings for him, some sort of feeling that she didn't want to examine at length, in any way, so no, this wasn't about Lincoln possibly fucking anyone else. It was about him disrespecting her as his teacher. Fuck this guy, she decided just before the DJ talked Kitty off the stage and called Roxie's name.

The number was supposed to be hot, enticing, and riveting, but Roxie knew it somehow turned out sad instead, mournful even. The performance probably downright sucked, she decided, as her leg caught too soon around the pole just as she was trying to do a graceful dive down. Her head fell back so fast it banged against the pole, but she ignored it and kept moving.

She just wanted to get this over with, get out of the place, and not speak to Lincoln again tonight. She'd blow up at him if he came near her, she knew it. Best to skip out on the rest of the night, even if she caught hell from Emily tomorrow for doing that. Kitty had to wait for Roxie to get done before she could leave, unless she called a cab. So once the performance was finished, Roxie went back to their changing room to tell the other woman they were leaving early. Only Kitty wasn't there.

Roxie fumed quietly in the room and waited, but an hour passed before Kitty finally saw Roxie's message and answered her. Roxie sighed with relief when Kitty walked in, ready to go. "You're missing a great party. Oh, and people loved us. I got so many cards from wives that want us for their events, it's crazy! Look."

Kitty all but bounced as she held out a stack of cards for Roxie to inspect.

"That's great, honey, but I need to go. Do you want to come with me or are you okay with taking a cab? I'll pay for it." Roxie already had her bag over her shoulder, the soiled dress inside ready for Wendy's tender loving care. Roxie had dressed in a black tank top and a pair of black shorts when she changed, hoping Kitty wouldn't be long.

"Oh, I'll take a cab, no worries. This party is the bomb, I'm not ready to leave yet, and the sitter will be there until midnight. And no, I'll pay for the cab, honey. Go take care of whatever's wrong. Text me if you want me, okay?" Kitty leaned over to kiss Roxie's cheek.

"Sounds fair. I'll give you a buzz tomorrow to check

you got home alright." Roxie always did that when one of her friends was staying somewhere she was leaving.

Roxie was about to start the car and pull out of the resort when her phone buzzed with a tone it didn't often buzz with. Nick was in town! Perfect. He could soothe her shattered nerves like no other could.

9

Roxie

Roxie turned the car engine off and poked buttons until she heard the phone ring. Calling Nick was better than a text any day.

"Hey, beautiful, how are you?" Nick's voice spoke from the phone with happy excitement. "You free tonight or do you have a hot date I have to compete with in order to get my fix?"

"Oh, you can have me all night, honey," Roxie said with a throaty laugh, forcing happiness into a voice that wanted nothing more than to pout. Nick was gorgeous, fun to be around, and always made her feel better, no matter how far down in the dumps she was.

"Well then, let me take you out to eat, if you haven't had dinner yet. Got any suggestions?"

"Hmm, how about cheap and cheerful? TGI Friday out by North Kings Highway?" She offered, knowing he'd have preferred something quiet, expensive, and intimate, but that wasn't what she felt like right now. She wanted a place where she could have a drink, laugh, and not ponder what it meant that Lincoln had brought another woman to the event without letting her know. She didn't want to end up in tears that would only add more rain to her parade, after all.

"That's fine, I know you don't care about eating at fancy places, so yeah, I'll meet you there in fifteen minutes, shall I?"

"That's a plan." She agreed and hung up the phone. She hadn't seen Nick since the fire at Elmo's so this was a treat for her. She'd met him a while back and though it was obvious he was interested in her - he made no bones about that at all - he didn't do it in a way that was creepy. On top of that he was supportive, funny, and most of all, loyal. That was hard to come by these days.

The fact that the man was a lookalike for Alexander Skarsgard and one of the richest men on the planet didn't phase Roxie. She knew hundreds of handsome men with money. Nick was the marrying kind that didn't fool around with dating. Once he found someone he liked, he pursued them with the idea of marriage in his mind. Which was why he didn't just go out on dates with dozens of women at a time, he was in it for the long haul. It was too bad he was so focused on her, she thought as she pulled into the parking lot of the restaurant she'd chosen. There were so many other women out there that would love to have him.

"Hey." She smiled as she opened the door and found Nick there waiting for her. She spotted his Maserati MC20 a few cars down and admired the car for a moment before she turned back to him. "I still love that car."

"If only you'd marry me for it," Nick said teasingly, but took her hand with a wide grin to let her know it was only a joke. "Let's eat. Catch up, what have you been up to?"

"Well, I guess you know Elmo's burned down, and all of us have been making ends meet however we can." She paused while a hostess took them to a table and ordered their drinks. Once the woman was gone she picked back up where she'd left off. "Oh, my boyfriend, ex-boyfriend I should say, is wanted for that fire, but he's missing, and oh, that was a lot to drop on you wasn't it?"

Roxie finally noticed the stunned look on Nick's face and her words dwindled off. His eyes went tmide for a moment before he spoke. "Wow, yeah, that's a lot. But you're single now, that's a good thing."

Roxie was about to tell Nick that she wasn't quite single, but decided against it when an image of Naomi smiling up at Lincoln in his playroom popped into her head. "I suppose I am."

A client was not a boyfriend, she reminded herself and took a sip of the Long Island Iced Tea the waitress brought to her. They ordered a lot of food they could nibble at and eat with their hands and were soon back as they usually were, smiling and laughing with each other.

Nick could always put Roxie at ease and tonight was no different. When they finished their food, Nick asked if she'd like to do anything else. Roxie looked over at him across the table and clenched her teeth in thought. Could she do it? Could she sleep with him?

It wouldn't be a simple matter of a quick fuck to Nick, if she went through with it, it would mean something to him. He'd always made his feelings clear to her and maybe he was the right choice. Especially if Lincoln was just going to prance around with Little Miss Holly-wood Actress at public events. She stared at him, adoring his blond hair, Nordic blue eyes, and six-foot-five-inch height. The man was a Viking giant, but as gentle as a lamb with her.

Maybe he was the one and she was too stupid to see that.

"Let's go back to your place. We can watch some movies and tear them apart. That's always my favorite thing to do with you." It was also when she felt the safest, when it was just the two of them, closed away from the world.

She'd had less of that time when she started dating Nathan, and because Nick's business took him off on trips all over the world, but he was here now. Spending some time with him would be nice.

"That sounds like a plan, meet you there, or do you want to ride with me?" He winked at her and she couldn't help but smile. He knew she loved his car.

"I'd love to have another ride in her, but I'll follow you in my old banger." Roxie pointed her thumb at the older model compact SUV behind her and shrugged. "A girl always needs to be able to pick up and go, you know?"

She laughed at the way her sentence rhymed and he smiled with her. "That's what I love about you, Rox, you never take yourself too seriously."

"Is that all it takes? I can give you a lot more reasons than that." She teased but his face moved into something enigmatic, hard to read.

"No, that's not all. But let's get going, shall we?" He pushed through the moment and she let it go.

Once they were settled into his penthouse, high above everybody else in Myrtle Beach, Roxie settled in, took her shoes off, and relaxed for the first time in what felt like months. "God, I'm glad you're home, finally."

Nick brought out two beers and set them on the

table before he sat down beside her on the luxurious black leather sectional in his living room. "Why's that?"

"Oh, you know." She scoffed and pushed up to reach for her beer. "I know I can count on you to be there when I need someone to listen. I have Emily, the girls I work with, and Wendy, but you're on the periphery of all of that and I know you'll set me straight if I'm wrong or tell me if I'm right."

"That's what friends are for, isn't it?" He asked, but she could see in his eyes that he wanted to be more than friends.

Normally, she could put his desire to the back of her mind. Normally, Nick did the same. But right now? Right now, it was burning out of those blue depths like ice blue flames.

Roxie, for reasons she could never fully explain, leaned into that look, leaned into his full lips. Her hand came up, cupped the left side of his face to hold it still, and did the unthinkable. She kissed him.

It was an innocent kiss, at first. It was meant to be an exploration, but then Nick groaned deep in his throat, a sound that always made her knees weak when men did it, and pulled her over his lap. Luckily, she'd changed into a pair of denim shorts earlier, but still, there wasn't much between their bodies when she sank down onto him.

"Roxie." He murmured against her jaw, "I've wanted you for far too long."

She hushed him up by taking his face in her hands and kissing him again. *Don't speak,* she thought to herself, *don't make me think of someone else.*

His hands came up to bury themselves in her hair and he groaned again. But maybe that was because her tongue snaked out, parted his lips, and then danced against his. His hands immediately came down to cup her ass, hold her tight against his hips where the undeniable proof of how much he wanted her was already more than obvious.

She wasn't thinking, wasn't even really feeling in that moment, she just wanted to lose herself in him. He pulled off her shirt and was about to pull aside the lace panels of the top she wore beneath, eager to taste her, but sensibility washed over her like ice water. "Nick."

"Don't make me stop, Roxie. I've wanted you for so long." Nick begged, but she shook her head and stood up.

"No, it wouldn't be right. I'd just be using you for sex and we're more than that, Nick. You're my friend." *Like a brother,* were the words she left unspoken. He knew it though and closed his eyes.

He inhaled deeply, looked around the living room he'd decorated like he'd bought everything at a Moroccan bazaar—there was even a black and ivory hookah in one corner—and swiped at his face. "You're right. I'd love to make you my wife, give you everything you've ever dreamed of, but I know that's not how you feel about me. I'd be taking advantage if I pressured you into anything more than being my friend."

"Thanks." Roxie rolled her eyes at herself and sat back down. "You totally took the blame for me making a pass at you."

"It's the gentlemanly thing to do, isn't it?" He wiggled his eyebrows and she couldn't help but laugh with him.

"If you say so." She pulled his arm over her shoulders and snuggled into his chest. "Tell me what you've been up to. Was it China you went to this time?"

"No, Egypt, to pick some new products out for my rare antiques shop in London. Then Turkey for the rare manuscripts shop in Paris. And a quick trip to Serbia to visit a friend before I came back here." He picked up the remote, but he didn't turn the TV on. "I'd like things to be different between us, Roxie, but I know what you need from me is friendship. Maybe one day things will be different, but for now, being your friend is acceptable."

"Good." She paused, then looked up at him. "Did you find any of those dresses we talked about the last time you were here? The caftans?"

"I did, and I will give them to you later. For now, let's just watch some trashy movies and have a drink." He flicked the TV on then, putting the matter to rest immediately. He'd said what he wanted to say and that was enough for him.

Roxie didn't push it, they both knew her heart wasn't in the right place and that was good enough. She couldn't even bring herself to tell him about Lincoln. Even if that man was the reason she needed Nick's friendship so much tonight. Nick knew all of her friends, she'd even told him about a few of her clients, but she didn't say a peep about Lincoln.

That was worrisome for a thousand reasons, but she didn't want to face any of them so she kept her mouth shut and let him choose a film to watch. He picked out one about some woman in England finding a Viking boat in her backyard during World War II. It was more interesting than she'd thought it would be but when her eyes grew heavy, she couldn't fight to keep them open.

She felt much too safe for the first time in months, much too comfortable to fight the sleep that pulled at her with heavy arms. There was no Nathan calling her a whore here, no men stalking her to get to Nathan here, and certainly no Lincoln driving her crazy with his mercurial moods to put her on edge.

Though to be fair, Lincoln was a lot calmer at his house, and a lot nicer than he was at his office. He wasn't such a dick at home, but mmm, she loved his dick. Her mind drifted off into blankness for the longest time as sleep took her. She didn't feel it when Nick slid out from under her, or when he picked her up and put her in a bed. She had no clue when he turned out the light and left the room either. She slept, deep, peaceful, and without nightmares.

She woke up sometime before dawn fully broke, but still felt rested. After a good stretch and quick trip to the bathroom, she gathered her shoes, left Nick a note on his fridge, and drove back to the motel. It had been a good night, a fun night, followed by some much-needed rest. She'd almost fucked things up when she made a pass at him, but oh well. That was the kind of friend Nick was, the kind that forgave easily.

What she was going to do about Lincoln slipped from her mind as she drove back to the hotel she called home for now. For the first time in over a week, she didn't even check all her mirrors as she drove. She just enjoyed the cool morning air from her open window and watched the sunrise. The smell of saltwater and hot tarmac might be gross to some, but to Roxie, it smelled like freedom.

Sure, Myrtle Beach was a summer town, a place for tourists to let go and act like idiots, but to her, it was home now. It was thousands of miles away from the life she'd left behind, the memories she left behind, but it was the place that let her do that. No questions asked, no explanations needed.

Now, if only she could approach this situation with Lincoln the same way. She pulled into her allotted parking spot and let herself into her room on the ground floor. Lincoln would never fit into this kind of place, but then, the Chloe she used to be wouldn't have either. Life had a way of hardening you like that, bringing out the best and worst as it saw fit. Maybe she needed to approach this thing with Lincoln much harder than she had been, she thought as she flopped down onto her springy bed. Maybe he needed to know that the sweet little sub could be one hard bitch to deal with when she was pissed off. Because, apparently, he hadn't figured that part out yet.

With a smug smile that could beat Lincoln's any day of the week, Roxie leaned back and started to plan. She'd have him on his knees promising to never see another woman again before she was through with him.

10

Lincoln

*L*incoln didn't usually worry about what a woman thought about him, or if she thought about him at all, but since that night of the charity event all he'd got from Roxie were short texts and no phone calls. He wasn't sure what the problem was, but he knew something wasn't right. Not that he called her to find out anything either.

He had to fly back to New York to settle some business up there, but he was only gone for two days. He arranged to meet with her when he got back mid-week and really didn't think too hard about it. She was a woman, a lot of shit was happening in her life, so she probably had things to deal with that didn't include him.

If she wanted to talk to him about it, he'd be glad to listen, but he wasn't going to push her right now.

She was the kind of woman who knew what she wanted out of life and worked hard to get it. Having a man pushing her to talk about her thoughts and feelings was probably the last thing she wanted. And not a part of their contract, as he could clearly hear her say in his head. When she wasn't at his place by 5:30 he sent her a text demanding to know where she was.

It took her fifteen minutes to reply but when she did, he frowned.

"Pick me up at my place. I have something in mind."

Mysterious. He liked mysterious. Especially when he knew Roxie's ideas always led to something fun. That made him smile as he pulled up to a parking spot outside her hotel and waited on her. What could she possibly have in mind tonight?

She came out the door before he'd even put the car into park, dressed in a slinky black dress shot through with silver threads. She wore a very nice pair of black stockings with two thick lines going up the back. He saw them when she turned to lock the door and his eyebrows lifted. He loved those stockings. No doubt about it.

She handed him a black mask as soon as she got in the car, a soft velvet number that would cover his eyes and nose and matched the one she had in her hand.

"What's this for?" He asked. He hadn't been expecting to take her out, but if that's what she wanted he'd take her wherever she wanted to go. Especially if it meant he'd get to look at the amazing cleavage she had on display.

"It's a surprise." She gave him a mysterious wink and put her seatbelt on.

"Okay, but I need to know the address at least."

"It's a private place, members only. Kind of like my old job."

She smiled the same as she always did, talked with ease, but something about her seemed brittle that he couldn't explain. Maybe she was nervous about being out with him, or maybe she'd just had a shitty day. She'd relax, he was sure of it.

"Oh, did you get that dress dry-cleaned? Naomi wanted to pay for it." He mentioned in an off-hand way as he pulled into traffic since she'd put the address into the GPS. He felt the way she went stiff and he could have sworn he heard her growl.

A quick glance showed she was staring through the windshield with studied aloofness. Fuck. What had he said wrong?

"I can afford to get my own dress dry-cleaned thank you."

Fuck! She'd taken it the wrong way. "She wasn't

suggesting you couldn't afford to, only that she felt responsible and wanted to pay for it."

That would help, right? Explanations always helped. Only this one seemed to make her jaw go hard and she sat up even straighter in her seat.

"It's taken care of." She waved further talk about it away and he decided to just let it drop.

"Okay." He swallowed and decided to focus on driving. She'd talk if she wanted to. Right?

He got into the groove of driving as The Cure sang about never-ending love on the radio. The GPS guided him soon enough to a place that looked like little more than a warehouse, but the glass reception area proved that wrong. A small sign on one panel of glass read "Skippers" in neon pink cursive, and Lincoln wondered what he was in for tonight. Was this some kind of upscale restaurant?

But why would he need a mask for that?

"As you're my guest and not a member, you have to wear the mask. I'm just wearing mine for the fun of it, but you have to keep yours on once we're inside." She went ahead and put her mask on, tying it so that the tie was hidden by her long hair. "Oh, we're here for 80s night, awesome."

Lincoln could only guess she knew that because Madonna was singing something about grooves. It was catchy but what caught his attention was the women dressed in scanty neon lingerie, walking around handing out drinks behind the doorman.

"Hi, Charlie, I've brought a guest tonight." Roxie walked right up to the guy, passing a line of people who glared at her.

Lincoln had hurried to put his mask on and caught up with her now. He noticed how the doorman treated her like she was a superstar and the waves she caught from some of the women walking around in heels and electrifying outfits. Some of the men were even dressed in vintage suits with razor-thin ties and their hair slicked back in an obvious 80s fashion.

Lincoln had changed into a fresh suit before he left the house to pick up Roxie. If he'd known there was a theme, he'd have worn something else, the suits might be vintage, but they were also designer vintage. Besides, he didn't care for wearing banana yellow suits, or thin ties. With a shrug he let her take his hand and guide him to a bar.

"So, it's a strip club?" He asked after she ordered them both drinks from a female bartender with hair teased super-high, dressed in a sequined red dress with huge shoulders.

"More than that, baby." She smiled that teasing, smug smile that only she could pull off. "So much more than that."

"A sex club?" This time he asked in a much quieter voice.

"Yep." She took the rum and coke the woman named Jill handed to her and slid over his double bourbon.

"I've been to both before, you know? All over the world."

"Right." She drew the word out as if she didn't believe him.

"I have. With clients." He twisted his neck, his shirt collar suddenly too tight. "It helps when you share the same interest as some of those clients."

"But I bet you never participated. Or took anyone off to a private room." She lifted her eyebrows in question, as if she already knew the answer.

And damn her, she probably did. He'd never been one to enjoy those places. He usually left well before his clients. In fact, usually as soon as the client disappeared, he'd make an exit without interacting with any of the girls available to him. It wasn't his thing.

But would it be different with Roxie by his side?

"I'll be gentle then, babe." She patted his hand and he looked down at her speculatively.

Was she really treating him like she had some kind of inside knowledge on him that he didn't know about himself?

A woman screeching and calling Roxie's name out

distracted him. Then a whole herd of men and women descended on them and one of the women drew Roxie out to dance on a dancefloor to the left of the bar. Lincoln laughed softly as Roxie let the woman draw her out, enjoying how carefree Roxie looked at that moment.

She danced like an expert, following the woman's lead as they danced to a slower song. It turned into a tango somewhere along the way, and Lincoln couldn't help but watch with fascination. She was good, no matter what kind of dancing she was doing. He saw the way it transported her, relieved all the tension in her body. It was hard to believe how open she became when she danced. Her every thought was displayed on her face as she wound her way through the dance with ease.

When she came back, barely out of breath, and asked if he was ready to go upstairs, he wanted to ask her for a dance of his own but decided against it. Maybe later.

"I have something special set up with the lady I was dancing with. Her name is Angelica, she's my girl from my days at Elmo's. She's here tonight with her dom. We're going to watch in their double room. Not partici-pate, though, just watch."

That made him swallow again, but this time it was because his throat was tight and dry. He sipped at the bourbon and let her lead the way. They rode the elevator up four floors and walked out to a long hallway with closed doors that bore symbols instead of letters.

He looked down at Roxie and saw her holding a red plastic triangle with a key attached by a metal ring.

Lincoln walked in after her, surprised to find that it wasn't the typical, double-bed hotel room that he'd expected. He closed the door to see a couple in the room already. The woman he'd seen downstairs, and a tall man that women would find handsome in that dark and broody kind of way.

Roxie tugged him over to a small couch against a wall, but Lincoln didn't take his eyes from the couple in the room. The woman must have raced up here after her dance with Roxie because she was now naked, her arms tied over her head to a ring around a pole.

"That's Angelica and her dom is Eric. He's pretty good but can go down dark paths." Roxie leaned over to whisper into his ear, her left hand on his right thigh. "If you get uncomfortable, just let me know. We can find something else to watch."

"I'm good." He said absently, his eyes still on the woman's body. She was tanned all over, perhaps Hispanic, with dark nipples that were very...suckable. Fuck, was he supposed to think about sucking another woman's nipples when he was with Roxie?

"She has a beautiful body, don't you think?" He heard her whisper again and relaxed a little. She was encouraging him to look, things were cool then.

The minutes passed with Eric teasing the woman

with words and soft touches as he tied ropes in knots around her body in intricate patterns. This was the rope-work Lincoln wanted to try his hand at. Angelica's head moved, following the caresses, clearly wanting more. Lincoln tried not to move too much but he was aroused already, and Roxie made it worse by moving the hand on his leg to his inner thigh. He wanted to tell her to stop but couldn't. It was too deliciously naughty, and he didn't want her to behave. Not really.

"Have you been a good girl, this week, pet?" Eric asked the smiling Angelica. Only, her face fell when he asked that and she looked down at her toes.

"No, Eric. I've been very bad, I'm sorry to say." Angelica pouted prettily, her dark eyes wide and bright. "I wanted to fuck Roxie when I danced with her earlier. I've had very lustful thoughts."

Lincoln's eyes shot to Roxie and saw that she was grinning. She liked knowing a woman wanted to fuck her. Okay, good to know. She was far more adventurous than he'd thought.

"Did you ask Roxie if you could think such things about her?" The man asked as he walked over to a chest of drawers to one side of the room. He drew out what looked like a very short whip with leather tongues.

"No, I didn't, Eric. I'm sorry, but I couldn't help myself. She's so fucking hot." The woman smiled a little in Roxie's direction but the smile vanished when the man came back with the whip.

"You know what happens when you're bad, don't you, Angelica? When you can't control yourself." The man stood with his feet planted a foot apart, his thick-muscled arms crossed over his chest.

"I do, Eric. But it's worth it. She's so beautiful." The woman looked at the man hopefully, but Lincoln suspected the plea was for the whip, not reprieve.

"She is beautiful, Angelica, but you were very bad. Turn around please."

Lincoln wasn't sure what to expect then, whether the man would use the whip on her right away or if he'd prolong this patter. Lincoln's eyes narrowed and he followed the man's movements as he walked behind the woman.

"Tell me what you thought, Angelica. All of it." He wrapped his arms around the naked woman, cupping her firm breasts gently. His fingers found the thick tips and plucked at them until the woman groaned and sank back against the man in surrender.

A sharp movement of his arm and a flick of his wrist brought the whip down on the woman's hip, catching her attention at once. Her eyes opened wide and she panted out an apology. "I'm sorry, Eric. I wanted to taste her on my lips. I wanted to feel her breasts in my hands."

"What else, Angel?" He drove her on, plunging the

handle of the whip between the woman's thighs to grind it there, against her cleft, until she was moaning in pleasure.

"I wanted her to touch me, to use her fingers on me. And maybe have you fuck me, Eric. You know I always want you."

"I do, Angel, but you're supposed to control these thoughts. You are supposed to only think of me unless I give you permission to think about another woman. Or man."

The man's eyes came up to Lincoln's and Lincoln froze.

"He wants to know if you want her. Just nod, but don't get up. This isn't our day to play with others."

Lincoln nodded, both at her and the man in the room. What the fuck had he gotten himself into here?

Lincoln

The night progressed and Lincoln was engrossed. The man was an expert at playing the role he'd taken on and Lincoln admired the skillful way he drew the woman's pleasure out while attaining his own. This was more than just bad girl punishment time, this was give and take.

Roxie continued to whisper things in his ear, directing his gaze or his thoughts to where she wanted them to go. He was about ready to jump off the couch, drag her to a room of their own, and reenact everything he'd just witnessed. He wanted to go through every moment he'd witnessed with her, but he was still too uncertain. Shy, even.

Lincoln watched, completely fascinated now that the

woman was on her knees, her back facing them. The man, Eric, was in front of her with his jeans open. The woman was obviously good at what she did because Eric was fighting fairly hard not to unload in her mouth. Lincoln knew all the signs of that problem and knew that if Roxie's hand went up his thigh, just a little bit further, he'd have the same problem as well.

He hadn't been this ready to blow so quickly since he was a virgin seeing his first pair of real breasts as a teenager. The sensation was a little embarrassing, but also very intriguing. Was he really turned on by the performance in front of him, or merely from the fact that he was watching two people go at it in real life?

"Let's go," Lincoln said suddenly and got up from the couch, his hand out to her.

"Wait, what?" Roxie whispered but followed his lead. This wasn't his room, and he knew the proper way to behave in this situation, even if he'd never been in it before. Luckily, Roxie did too.

"It's time to go."

"I'm not ready to go yet." She protested once the door was closed and they were headed for the elevator.

"It is." He had to get her home, to his own private playroom where he could do all of those things to Roxie without an audience.

"But we came here to play, Lincoln. This is your

lesson tonight." She dug her heels in as the elevator doors opened, her face set in protest.

"Nope, not tonight. That's not a lesson, Roxie. That's cheating, no better than watching a video online really. That's really lazy teaching." He nudged her into the elevator and for a minute he thought she'd protest again but something changed in her face.

"Well, perhaps if you'd participated a little more..." She goaded, her eyes impish and her mouth twisted in accusation.

"Making me watch people have sex is very unprofessional, Roxie. It deserves..." He paused when he saw a spark light up in her eye.

"It deserves nothing, take me home." She put her arms over her chest and lifted her chin as the elevator went down.

"I don't think so." He said it quietly but saw the way her eyes moved to look at him from the side, how her head tilted just a little. "I think I'll take you back to my playroom."

"You just try." She said, but she didn't run away when the doors opened. Instead, she followed him right out to the car, her hand in his.

Maybe that's what he'd been missing the last few times he'd been in the playroom with her. He needed to make her his, claim her. Even if it was a loose claim, he still needed to let her know that he'd claimed her. Okay, he understood now.

Roxie didn't say anything as he drove back to his house and let them in. She did strip off her dress as soon as she walked into the house, though. That was a good sign. She stopped when she'd made her way up to his playroom, clearly noting his new addition. A bed with an intricate ironwork headboard and iron posts at each corner.

"It caught my eye at an antique shop at home. I thought it was perfect for this room, don't you agree."

"It's lovely, Lincoln. It really is. I love the red sheets." There wasn't anything else on the bed for her to compliment. It was a bed for sex, not sleeping.

"Good. Get on it."

For a moment, he thought she'd balk, that she'd walk out, but she did as she was told. "Do you want me to strip completely?"

"No, I want to try some ropework tonight, so you can leave the top and stockings on." He went to the drawer where he'd stashed black velvet ropes earlier. He'd practiced with them the night before at his penthouse in New York, imagining how the soft, dark rope would look when it was knotted to hold up her breasts, or cascading down her abdomen, then between her thighs. The fantasies had nearly driven him to order a plane right away and leave the city, but he'd managed to contain himself. Watching the man do some of the very ties he'd practiced, expertly and with skill, Lincoln knew he had to try them tonight. And if it meant claiming Roxie in the process, well, two birds, one stone.

"Right arm, please." He asked, but it came out as more demand than request.

She held her hand out and he fumbled with the knot for a moment. It wasn't just the standard tie two ends together and go kind of knot, it was an intricate hold that involved wrapping the rope around and then creating a cinch that would hold. At first, he thought he'd fuck it up and Roxie was looking at him doubtfully.

"Come on, admit it. You practiced this shit with Naomi the other night, didn't you?"

Lincoln paused as he finally got the knot tied. "What?"

"Naomi? Your little TV star. I'm sure she's the adventurous kind that likes being tied up by a man. In fact, why am I even here?" She got up but had to sit right back down because her right arm was tied to the bed. "For fuck's sake."

"No, Rox. No. But yeah. Um, what the fuck?" Lincoln stared at her, completely floored about what he'd just heard. "Okay, Naomi's hot, beautiful, but she's gay, Roxie. She's playing for the other team. Not interested in any man, even me, and believe me that's fucked up because I'm hot as fuck."

He tried to play it off with a joke, but yeah, that shit kind of stung when she told him. Roxie didn't laugh, her eyes narrowed and she tilted her head. "She's what now?"

"Gay, Roxie. Naomi is gay. There's nothing going on between us. No matter what you might think. She's not interested in men at all. I've known her for years and she's in a relationship with a woman, but they keep it quiet, so that doesn't leave this room, understand?" He stared down at her, hoping this was what had been bothering her and that they could finally get back on track.

"She's gay?" Roxie sat back against the headboard. "Gay?"

"Yes, Roxie, gay. All the way gay, not a little gay, but all the way gay." He took a deep breath. "I sometimes act as her date to throw off the homophobes for her. That's all that's between us. A lot of years of hanging out, going to ballgames when we're both in the same town, and an occasional event of some kind. I even went to the television sion awards show with her once."

"So, you didn't bring her back here to our, *your* play-room?" Roxie asked softly, as if the news wasn't sinking in at all for her.

"No, Roxie. She went back to her girlfriend at the resort that night. Otherwise, yeah, I might have. I have a hard time being just friends with straight women, even though I know tons of them. It might have been more if she wasn't gay, but she is, so yeah, we're just friends." He smiled at her and brushed a lock of hair behind her left ear. His fingers stroked at her jaw before he dropped his hand and just looked at her. "Are we good now?"

He could see her thoughts in the way she narrowed her eyes, not sure whether to believe him or not. Finally, she came to a decision and her face set in a determined look that made his blood surge all over again.

"Fine. Now do the other hand." She grinned as she rolled to her back and put her free hand up against the post. This time, Lincoln had no qualms about the tie. Roxie tried to direct him, but he ignored her until he had his ropes around her breasts. Then she very strictly told him what was too tight and what wasn't tight enough. "You can do some serious harm if you aren't careful, so keep an eye on my skin, and listen when I tell you something, alright?"

"Yes, but I'm the dom here, not you."

"I think you might have to fight me to prove it tonight, Lincoln." She murmured, clearly not cowed at all.

"I think I can change your mind for you." He went to the drawer, carefully looking at her to see her reaction. She looked like she was trying to pull off uninterested boredom but failed miserably at it. Her eyebrows lifted when he opened the drawer holding nipple stimulation tools. He drew out those wonderful purple suckers and placed one on each breast carefully. He had tied the ropes around her breasts to resemble a cupless bra, then continued down around her waist and around each thigh. She wasn't totally motionless, totally helpless, but she wasn't going anywhere soon.

"Now, tell me something, Roxie," Lincoln said as he came to the edge of the bed, a soft whip in his hand.

"Yes, Lincoln?" She asked, her eyes on the whip before they came up to accost his. He saw hope in her sultry blue eyes this time, a need to be conquered. He hadn't seen that in her gaze before and it thrilled him.

"What did you do while I was in New York?" He held the short whip in his hand, flicking it around to get the feel of it.

"I rode my bike to the stores, ate at the restaurant, and read a few books." She responded, confusion on her face.

"You didn't think about me?" His head tilted in question, not sure what he wanted her reply to be.

"Well, no, I thought you were here, fucking your TV princess." She sneered and looked away. He felt a pang of...enjoyment? Yes, enjoyment, knowing she was jealous, even if she chose to pretend to be angry instead.

"Ah, but you're the only princess I know, Roxie." He traced the tails of the soft leather whip along her toes, then up her legs. Teasing her, letting her know that he knew what to do with the tool. "Shouldn't you have asked me sooner? What was that you told me? We have to trust each other and without trust, this won't work? Isn't that what you told me?"

"Yes, it is what I told you, Lincoln." She answered, her eyes following the path of the whip, her face flushed from the efforts of the nipple suckers. When she moaned it was clearly involuntary, but then he'd pressed the hilt of the whip against her folds, so it wasn't a surprise.

"And do you promise to trust me from now on?" He asked, moving the whip away to run the tails over her firm breasts.

"I do, Lincoln. I do." She panted the words, and he was drawn down to the bed, too caught up in how aroused she was to ignore his own body's need to be next to her. His fingers traced down her silky thigh, over her flat stomach, before going back down to the place he'd dreamed of every night since he'd last been with her.

"Are you sure, Roxie? Do you think you'll get upset like that again if you see me with another woman?" It finally occurred to him what she'd admitted, a weakness, that she was upset because she thought he was fucking another woman. She'd been upset. The ice princess who didn't feel anything had been…jealous. That was progress.

"I promise, Lincoln." She answered, but he still didn't believe her. Not yet.

"Let me help you roll over." He tugged on the knots, running out more rope so she could turn over. To her hands and knees.

She didn't try to take control or move away, she simply took the help he offered and knelt as he instructed her to do. He teased them both once he'd undressed and put a condom on. He pushed his cock against her, but not inside of her. He wanted to be sure she meant what she'd promised.

"Are you sure, Roxie?"

"Yes, Lincoln. Please fuck me." She ground out the words, as if angry. Her back was taut, not an image of submission at all. But those stockings on her legs were a picture he'd never forget.

"Roxie?"

"Yes, Lincoln?" She almost purred his name when he moved his cock to tease her opening.

"You aren't ready yet. You don't mean it." With that, he reached around to press a finger against her clit. To circle it in a way he knew she loved.

"Of course, I do!" She moaned, but she hadn't made that sound yet. That sweet sound of frustrated need that signaled she was about to take matters into her own hands.

"No, I don't think you do, Roxie." He moved down

behind her to swipe his tongue over her glistening folds, pushing her torso down to aim her ass higher. "I'll know when you're really ready."

His next swipe produced a keening sound, something new that he'd never heard her make before.

"Lincoln." He heard her gasp his name and wondered if now was the moment. "Please Lincoln, I need you inside of me."

"Hmm, maybe." He replied without moving away from her, he just kept stroking her skin with his tongue. Her hips moved in time with his tongue, telling him she was enjoying every moment of this most intimate attention. A thick finger slid into her opening produced a clench from her that nearly made him lose his own control.

"You have to fuck me, Lincoln. Now." This came out as a growl, almost guttural. The sound of a tigress warning her prey she's about to attack.

That was the sound he'd been waiting on. One final check of the condom he'd put on, and he plunged into her with one sure thrust. Almost immediately she started to pulse around him, her hips pounding against his. Lincoln's strong hands took over when he grasped her hips and held her still to thrust into her roughly, hard and fast the way her body demanded him to. It was rough, wild, and perhaps still a little vanilla compared to what he'd witnessed earlier, but this was progress.

With one final thrust, Lincoln let his control slip and followed Roxie into oblivion. Later, he'd worry about why he couldn't get enough of her when he could fuck other women once and forget them. Later he'd worry about why he wanted to explore her body, her mind, even more than they'd explored already. Later, much later, he'd worry about why he was already thinking about renewing the contract for much longer than a month. Much later.

12

Roxie

"How am I supposed to get through my life knowing I actually like this fucking man?" Roxie asked the empty, barebones bathroom of the hotel room she'd occupied since Nathan trashed her house. It still felt wrong going back there, so she was still here despite the fact that Lincoln had offered her a room at his place, and despite the fact that she hadn't seen a hint of those awful men anywhere near her.

Sometimes it was easy to forget there was a threat against her out there, lurking in the dark corners of the world she inhabited. Sometimes it was easier to remind herself of that than to examine her feelings for Lincoln. Staring into her own eyes in the mirror, a swipe of makeup setting spray drying on her face, Roxie let herself be distracted from the most immediate problem she faced.

A knock on the door reminded her why Lincoln was her most immediate problem. A frown creased her features, but she smoothed it out before she opened the door. "Hi. Come in?"

"Yeah, sure. Everything alright?" He seemed nervous, even though he was only there to pick her up to go to his place.

"Yeah, it's all good." Holy fucking moly, she lied so easily it even astonished her sometimes.

"Do you have a passport?" Rather than his usual smooth, calm approach to life, Lincoln seemed nervous. That put her even more on edge.

"Why?" She frowned again, her left eyebrow going up.

"Well, I need to go to Cambodia. I thought I'd take you with me." He smiled uneasily as if he knew the answer already. But then, he did, didn't he?

"You know I don't do dates, Lincoln. Not with clients. Going to clubs, *adult* activities, that's one thing. But dates? No." She shook her head for emphasis and crossed her arms under her breasts in a stance of strong denial. Her hair shimmered around her shoulders in black and purple waves, as if it too was denying him the chance at a date.

"This isn't really a date, though, Rox." Lincoln sat

down on the one chair in the room, an avocado green easy chair that must have come from a 1970s horror yard sale. It was comfortable, though.

"What is it then?" Her chin came up as she inspected him for any hint of a lie.

"It's a humanitarian trip. I've been sponsoring a village there for the last three years, helping them build housing and infrastructure of that nature. There was a storm last week and a lot of the houses were damaged. I need to go and inspect the damage. The plan is to work with them for the next fifteen years, but this storm might have set them back a year or two." He shrugged, held out his hands with the palms up, and looked at her with a plea in his eyes. "I thought you'd like to go, get out of the States for a while. Maybe work with the kids some? I'll be gone for a week or two so, um…"

"You'd miss me?" She asked, feeling something cold and hard unthaw in her chest a little. She didn't want to feel the warm and fuzzies for this man, but damn if he didn't have a way of making her do just that.

"A little." He replied with a 'not really' expression on his face that she didn't believe. He would miss her. Damn.

"Uh. I need to check and see if it's still valid. You know what it's like getting a passport these days." Roxie muttered, totally unsure if the fake passport she had would get her through the airline inspection and security or not. She'd never used it since she got it a few years back, hoping to take a trip to Mexico that hadn't panned out because of a hurricane.

"Of course. And I'd pay for everything, airfare, hotel, all of that."

"You don't have your own private jet yet, Lincoln?" She sat down on the bed, giving him an innocent smile that was anything but. She was teasing the hell out of him and the way his right eyebrow rose on his forehead told her he knew it.

"No, I don't see the point when there are so many commercial flights available. I don't fly often enough here in the States to justify one, and well, I can just borrow one from my stepdad if I need to." He said, but then looked at her, as if afraid the mention of someone from their past would upset her.

"I see. I'm glad you're still in touch with him." She wasn't sure what else to say to that. The mention of Dr. Bennet didn't bother her, mainly because she'd become adept years ago at not thinking too hard about people from her past. "So, when are you leaving?"

"Tomorrow, if we can manage it." He inhaled deeply and looked around the room, not in judgment, though. He was simply observing where she spent a lot of her time.

"I'll get Wendy to get it from her parent's safe and

have her bring it to me." She said before she could think too long about not going on the trip.

"You'll go then?" Lincoln's smile lit up the dim quiet of the room, a megawatt sign of happiness.

"Sure. I think. Like I said, I'll have to check the expiration date." She knew that was fine, she just had to worry about whether the ID she'd bought from a dealer Wendy knew was good enough to pass inspection. She'd paid enough for the damn thing.

"Great, does that change our plans for tonight then?"

"No, we're still on for dinner. I'll have Wendy meet me at your place, if that's alright?" She picked up her bag and her phone and moved towards the door.

"Yeah, sure, that's great." He still seemed nervous, but happy now, at least.

"Good. I'll just message her." Roxie spoke as she tapped a text into her phone.

They got in Lincoln's car and he drove while she stared at her phone.

Wendy, sweet, innocent Wendy, wasn't as sweet as her parents thought she was. Nor as innocent as she appeared to be either. She knew people from her parents' sphere, both in their community life and from the dry-cleaning shop, that weren't exactly on the up and up. One of those people had helped Roxie get the government-issued identification with fake paperwork that had her real fingerprints and other biometric data on it. It had cost a fortune and Roxie could only hope it worked. Otherwise, this little foray into a foreign country might cost her everything. Fuck, this was too deep.

"Are you sure that passport won't get me arrested?" She asked once Wendy responded, saying she'd bring it over to Lincoln's house.

"They're good. A friend went down to Argentina last year for a cousin's wedding and had no problems at all. You'll be fine, I promise." Wendy replied quickly.

"I hope so. I can't believe I'm doing this." Roxie typed, side-eyeing Lincoln to make sure he couldn't see what she'd written.

"I can't either, but maybe it'll be good for you. Get you out of here for a while."

"I thought about that, too," Roxie replied, staring through the windshield.

Then she asked Lincoln; "What's it like in Cambodia? All I know about it is some of the history of the place and something about the Vietnam War, and not much else." Roxie felt stupid asking but it wasn't a place that had been on her radar. The trip there would take a long time, she was certain.

"It's a nice place to visit, if you're a tourist. It's pretty hard to get by if you live there, though." Lincoln changed lanes to turn in the direction of his house. "We'll fly out to California, take another flight from there to Singapore. Once we're in Singapore, I'll have to charter a private jet to get us to Cambodia."

"Sounds exhausting." She answered, thinking about all those trips up and down in different planes. It wasn't one of her favorite ideas, flying. Still, she'd get to go somewhere completely different and that was exciting.

"It can be, yes. Even flying first class can leave you exhausted after so many planes." He stopped when he pulled into his driveway and put the car in park while the security gate closed behind them. "Did you send Wendy the gate code?"

"Yeah, she'll be here in a half-hour or so." Roxie nodded and walked behind him as they headed into the house. The scent of vanilla and oranges hit her gently, but she liked it.

"I'm going to order some food for dinner. Anything you want? Anything special for Wendy?"

They settled on what food to order while Roxie sat down on the couch in the living room she'd decorated. She wore a slip-dress with sandals today, nothing fancy, just easy to get out of. She wanted to lean back and panic about going on a trip with Lincoln, about getting arrested if they figured out her passport was fake, about why she'd agreed to all of this when that could very well happen. Instead, she made her mind go blank and forced herself to relax. It was something she'd learned long ago when she was nervous for a ballet recital. She perfected it when she'd taken on her first client at Elmo's. The guy had been gorgeous, gentle, and kind, but still, she'd been nervous.

Not unlike Lincoln in some ways. Lincoln was normally assertive, in control, and demanding, but he wasn't unkind. Since she'd taken him on as a student, he'd been nervous, tentative, hesitant even, but that had changed since she'd taken him to that sex club. He was learning to be more confident, more in control, and since he'd explained about Naomi things had changed.

She'd wanted to show him who was boss when she took him to that sex club, but he'd shown her instead, and that had surprised her. Oh, it had pleased her too, but it was a surprise that he'd caught on at last. Roxie wasn't the kind to give in easily and with Lincoln, everything had become more difficult. His taking charge had made that a lot easier, even if he was still tentative about some things. Like this crazy trip he'd proposed to her.

Holy fucking moly, what had she got herself into, she silently screamed in her head while pulling her hair back from her face. This was the very definition of insanity, doing something this stupid. And not just because she might end up in jail. She'd be very alone, very dependent on Lincoln and that was even crazier than going to jail as far she was concerned. Being dependent on any man was not something she was comfortable with.

"Stop freaking out, girl." Wendy's voice broke through Roxie's little crisis moment.

"You're here. Cool. We ordered enough food for you if you want to stay for dinner."

"Awesome, you know I'd never turn down food. I do have somewhere to be later, but it's not for a few hours." Wendy waved her hand around as if to brush aside any questions. "What did you order for me?"

"Well, it's from that Mexican cantina, what do you think I ordered you?" Roxie smiled, knowing just about every food that was Wendy's favorite dish from each culture.

"Oh my, did you order extra salsa and guacamole? You know I love that place. Their burritos are the bomb. Literally." Wendy snickered at her own joke, meaning the food caused her a lot of gas later, but it was worth it.

"Yes, we ordered extra everything. Come on, let's have the passport." Roxie held out her hand for the ID and stared at it with intensity once Wendy gave it to her. "I can't tell the difference between mine and yours, other than the identifying information."

"They look the same when they're scanned too. The guy has an inside connection where they print these off. I don't know." She paused to shrug before she went on, her face graced with a wry smile. "I guess being a government employee doesn't pay enough. Like I said, I don't know, I just know they're the best you can get."

"The best what?" Lincoln came in with several bags in his hands.

Roxie hadn't even heard the delivery car pull in, but she wouldn't complain about the food arriving. "Nothing, just talking about stuff from her work."

Wendy looked at Roxie in question but kept her mouth shut. Roxie didn't want Lincoln to know her passport was fake. Sure, he knew her identity as Roxie was fake, but he didn't have to know her passport wasn't real either.

"Let's eat. Oh, got our tickets organized, and Tanya's working on the rest of it for us. We leave around lunchtime tomorrow." Lincoln left the room to head for the dining room.

"Let's get plates and stuff," Roxie said, sliding the passport into her handbag before she left the room. "I might have a heart attack before the morning comes, worrying about this, so I might as well enjoy some Mexican food before I die."

"Not a bad decision. Are there any margaritas by any chance?" Wendy asked, following behind Roxie.

"I'll make us some. Might as well end the night drunk too, right? Although, having a hangover on a plane is probably a bad idea." Roxie mused and Wendy rolled her eyes.

"It's the worst, not recommended, two thumbs down. No drunk for you tonight girl. You're on your way to Cambodia, whether you like it or not." Wendy laughed as they entered the dining room and Lincoln looked up with a grin.

"I think she'll love it if she'll just give it a chance." Lincoln didn't frown or look upset, Roxie saw, but he wasn't the kind to be easily offended.

She watched him when she came back from making three margaritas and wondered just how stupid she was to agree to this crazy idea. And what did it mean about her feelings for him? Holy fuck.

"Oh, by the way, there's a change in our flight time tomorrow. I hope you're good at 4 am." Lincoln looked at her with brows knitted in worry.

"It's not my favorite time of the day, but I'll cope," Roxie answered, wondering if she'd sleep at all.

13

Roxie

*R*oxie stared out at the small airport, utterly, totally exhausted. They'd left Myrtle Beach at 5 am the day before. Or was it two days before? It might have even been three, she wasn't certain now. They'd stopped in Charlotte, North Carolina waiting for the plane that would take them to Los Angeles. That flight had left at almost 10 am and arrived in California at a little past 12 pm.

That totally boggled her brain, even knowing it was the time zone differences that made a nearly five-hour flight turn into two. Unfortunately, there was only one flight out of LAX to the airport in Singapore, and that included a stop in San Francisco. Tanya had scheduled their flight to San Francisco for the same day as they arrived in Los Angeles, which meant one more flight before she could finally be on solid ground again.

"I'm going to die if I have to take off in a plane one more time today, Lincoln." She mumbled as they disembarked. At least the passport had held up so far, she thought blearily as he pulled their carry-on luggage and gave her a smile that proved she wasn't the only one who was tired.

"You'll be able to rest once we get to the hotel for the night. I'll order room service once we get there." He kissed the top of her head when she stumbled into him and that felt…nice.

She was too tired to worry about anything else so she focused on putting one foot in front of the other until she saw a huge California king bed that couldn't have looked more inviting. She wanted to shower and wash off all the germs of being closed up with other people for most of the day, but collapsed when she drew near to the bed. "Fuck, this is heaven."

"I'll get us some food, Rox, relax," Lincoln said and closed the door to their room.

Some sexy time and hotel romp ideas flitted into her brain, but exhaustion took over and her eyes closed. She woke up later with Lincoln nudging her leg gently.

"Food's here if you want to eat." He smiled, lighting up the world for a moment. She couldn't help but smile back at him.

"Water?" She asked, her voice tight and dry.

"Lots of it, come on, I'll help you get there." He tugged at her hand and helped her stumble over to the chair.

"I can't believe how tired I am." She blinked down at the food on the table, glad he'd ordered her a simple steak with mashed potatoes and a salad. She couldn't have dealt with much more than that.

"I am too, but we have more traveling to do so eat up, then we'll change into our pajamas, put some horribly boring shit on TV to drown out any noise, and get to sleep." His eyes were taut around the edges and she could see he was as tired as she was.

"Sounds like a good idea." She had to agree, even if it wasn't quite past 6 pm yet.

She slept like a baby that night, and the next day they took off for Singapore. They had to stopover in Tokyo for an hour and arrived in Singapore where Lincoln told her the bad news. She was certain her face was going to just slide right off her skull, she was so sick of flying, but she took a deep breath.

"I know you're tired, and we've basically spent the last eighteen hours flying. I think we slept some on the plane last night from Japan to here, but well, there's one more flight." He wouldn't look at her. That was probably for the best. If she could muster up the energy she'd explode.

"One more flight?" She asked weakly, staring at him with one eye open before she closed that one too. Nope, not mustering the energy for an explosion at all. "One more flight. We can do this."

"It's just a little puddle jump across to Cambodia." He sighed and looked around, trying to find something, but she wasn't sure what.

"How long is a puddle jump exactly because I'm going to just lie down on the floor and die if it's as long as that last flight." She was miserable, growing cranky, and wishing terribly that she'd just stayed home now.

"Well, um, it's only two hours. But we can rest at one of the hotels here until tonight. The flights only go out late in the evening." He had the decency to look sheepish at least. She stared at him blankly before she spoke to him.

"Fine. Hotel. Now. Please." She walked away from him, heading for the exit and he had to jog to catch up to her to push her in the other direction, to where the actual exit was.

Another hotel swam into her world, with a dinner she wished she could remember but couldn't taste, and they were back at the airport. Roxie was still barely holding both her eyes open, but she hadn't had coffee yet. Luckily, she got a really shitty cup of pure caffeine on the plane and that had her wide awake when they landed in Phnom Penh at 8 pm local time. Roxie didn't even bother looking at her phone to find out what time it was at home. The device had updated the date and time as they landed at each new place and she couldn't even remember what day it was anymore anyway.

She looked around at what she could see of the small airport. It was so small she wasn't sure how it handled commercial flights at all, but she was there now. It was at least 80 degrees, even though darkness had fallen, and she wanted nothing more than AC. "Tell me we're done."

"Almost. We're staying at a hotel tonight, then traveling to the village tomorrow." Lincoln sighed, clutching her close to his side with an arm around her shoulders. "You've done great, Roxie. We're almost done."

"Thanks." She mumbled, wondering if she could just take up residence here and never get on a plane again.

The night turned into a blur and she opened her eyes the next morning to a smiling Lincoln with a cup of hot coffee in his hands. "Hi. Welcome to Cambodia."

"Thanks." She smiled and slid up in the bed, holding a sheet to her chest. "I guess I was too tired to do anything but strip off."

"We both were." Lincoln agreed and moved to pick up his own cup of coffee before he sat down on the bed with her. "Some of my team that work here will pick us up in two hours to take us the rest of the way."

"Oh?" She asked, not sure she wanted to hear the news.

"No planes, just a four-hour bus ride, and then we're done."

"Thank fuck." She thought back over the last few days, how she'd flashed that fraud of a passport without getting a second glance, and was relieved to know it had all worked. She was here at least. Exhausted, but here. "Then we get to work?"

"No, we'll meet, well, *I'll* meet up with the villagers and see what needs to be done first. I expect my team here will have all that information for me to look over once we're on the bus, but I'll make the final decision once we're there. You can rest if you want to."

"Cool." She sipped at her coffee and wondered what kind of hotel there'd be in the village.

"Great, I'll call for some breakfast."

Roxie took a quick shower, put her hair up in a knot, decided not to bother with makeup since the temperature was supposed to be in the 90s that day, and put on a pair of denim shorts and a loose black t-shirt. A pair of Skechers completed the laidback ensemble, and she came out of the bathroom ready for the day.

"You look great for a woman who's just traveled halfway across the globe," Lincoln said with an easy smile.

"Good answer, buddy. Good answer. Oh, breakfast looks nice." It was mainly fruit and some sweet bread, but she didn't care. Her stomach wasn't exactly happy and the fruit settled in her tummy nicely. An hour later they were downstairs, and Roxie couldn't take her eyes off Lincoln.

He wasn't in a suit and tie, or even trousers with a nice shirt. He was wearing black sneakers with a label she didn't recognize, a pair of khaki shorts, and a plain white t-shirt. He looked so…ordinary. Sure, he was gorgeous as fuck, but he didn't look…rich now. It suited him, she decided as a load of people on a bus got out and surrounded him.

She heard American accents and what was either British or Australian, or maybe both, as the group crowded around him. It was nice hearing the voices mix with the accents of the Cambodian people around them. Roxie had been surprised to learn that every Cambodian she interacted with spoke English very well and it was a relief to her at the same time.

"Shall we go, Lincoln? The village is waiting for us." A man with dark hair spoke and Lincoln turned to Roxie.

"Are you ready?" He asked, a huge grin shaking away any exhaustion he must have felt.

"As I'll ever be." She was glad Lincoln had advised her to bring normal, somewhat modest clothes, not fancy or skimpy stuff, because everyone that greeted them was dressed in shorts and t-shirts. Most wore sandals and hats too. There was a wide-brimmed hat in one of her bags, she'd have to dig that out later, she decided.

The first hours on the bus Roxie spent quietly watching the scenery go by. Lincoln was looking at videos his team had shot and reading over damage reports while they all strategized and worked together to come up with the best approach. When they'd come to some kind of consensus Lincoln joined her at the front of the bus.

"What do you think?" He asked as he slid into the seat beside her.

"It's so green. Everywhere, it's so green." She turned to smile at him. "And everybody waves."

"They do, yeah. It's one of the things I love about it here." He paused before he went on, as if trying to pull it all together in his brain. "I came here during my under-grad years, on a summer program. I decided then that I'd help the villagers somehow. I came up with this program when I found out the one I'd been on had lost most of the funding they needed. Kids come over on my program now, but I have a team here full-time, year-round. There's just some things I need to be here to approve, and it doesn't do me any harm to get my own hands dirty does it?"

"No, I suppose not." She gazed at him in wonder, proud that he'd spent one of his summers helping others. It made her decision to leave him all those years ago easier to think about now. If she'd stuck around, he'd never have gone on that trip, and well, it was best that he had. "I'm so proud of you, Lincoln. Even if I still hate you."

"It's okay, princess. You'll probably hate me forever. I can deal with that." He leaned over to kiss her cheek and smile at her.

"I hate you more after all those plane rides. And just wait until we get back home. It'll be pure raw hatred by then." She grinned and leaned into him, not meaning it at all. For a change.

"I don't doubt it a bit, Roxie. Not one bit." He put his right arm around her shoulders and held her close while the bus traveled on, until it finally stopped in a small village.

"This is it?" She asked, looking around. The drive had taken around four hours, but she had no idea where she was on the map. One of the women had said the name of the village but it didn't ring any bells for Roxie. For now, it didn't matter, they were sheltered under a canopy of tall trees and she could see the ocean out in the distance. A nice breeze blew around her, cooling her skin as she stepped off the bus.

She allowed the others to get off first, a little worried about how the villagers would greet her. She needn't have worried though, some women from the village came up to her with smiles and spoke to her.

"Hi, Lincoln said we're to make sure you get to your quarters. Could you follow us please?" The oldest one, in her late forties by the lines around her eyes, asked Roxie.

"Of course, just let me get the bags." Roxie started to agree but they waved her off.

"One of the children will bring those, don't worry. Come with us please."

"It's nice to meet you both, I'm Roxie." She introduced herself, liking them both instantly. There was a family resemblance and Roxie wondered if they were mother and daughter.

"I'm Chantou and this is my daughter, Chantavy." The older woman explained. "It's very nice to meet you too."

"Thanks," Roxie answered and followed along to what looked like military tents. She'd only ever seen them on television or in movies, but the boxy forest green tents were large enough to move around in and store things if need be. Not the hotel she'd hoped for, but she wouldn't complain. "This looks great."

"It's not a hotel, but all the people from Lincoln's program use these. Is it okay?" Chantou asked, her much shyer daughter happy to dissolve into the background.

"It's fine, really." Roxie sat down on the single bed arranged in the corner of the tent and wondered how she'd fit into the bed with Lincoln in it. "Is there somewhere we can get something to drink?"

"Oh, my son is bringing some juice and water. It will be here soon. After Lincoln is finished, we'll meet in the town hall and have lunch together." Chantou informed her and Roxie nodded her head.

"Great. Want to show me around?" Roxie couldn't think of anything better to do than to get stuck right into life here. It was helpful that both women spoke English and seemed nice. For now, getting her brain around time zones, schedules, and everything else would have to wait. She had to find her footing, then she could deal with that.

14

Roxie

oxie hadn't seen Lincoln since they shared a dinner with the villagers. She was exhausted from the long trip across the globe and had excused herself once she'd finished her meal. The people that surrounded her were all nice and friendly, from the villagers to the team that stayed there full-time to work. They'd accepted her excuse with knowing but understanding smiles.

She was so tired that she felt out of place, and even though everyone spoke to her in English, she felt rude for not knowing a single word of the language. *Typical American tourist* kept running through her brain when she could function enough to form a thought. Going to bed would sort that out.

The tent was still warm inside, despite the fact that darkness had fallen. A white slip of a nightgown was all she could bother to put on, anything else would be far too hot for her. Roxie hated to sleep when it was as hot as this, but she was in desperate need of some downtime. She'd picked up her phone to see if she could read herself to sleep on her book app but heard a noise outside.

"Hello?" She called out, tense in the confines of a tent that had no solid door or walls to keep intruders out. But there was no electricity, only battery-powered lanterns that had small solar panels on them, and that was a good thing as far as she was concerned. Even if she couldn't charge her phone.

"It's just me. I came to check on you and bring you some mosquito spray. You might want to spray yourself and the netting over your bed." Lincoln said once he'd opened the flap to come inside.

"Oh, good. Sorry, I'm so tired that I couldn't stay at the dinner any longer." She sat down on the small bed and suddenly felt very...lonely. "Did they give us separate tents for a reason, Lincoln? Like, is it taboo for us to sleep together here?"

"It is frowned upon for unmarried couples to live together, yes." Lincoln looked around sheepishly, his cheeks a little pink. "But, uh, I could stay with you for a while. We're foreigners so they probably wouldn't say anything, but I don't want to cause problems if I can avoid it."

That made her smile. He was so cute when he was being shy like that while also being so respectful of the people here. "I understand. I'd like you to stay with me for a while if you can. I've gotten used to sleeping beside you over the last few days and I think I'd miss you being with me."

"Oh. Are you sure?" His smile was like a reward that soothed her even more.

"I'd love it if you would." She looked down at her small bed and then back at Lincoln, wondering if they'd both fit. "I'm sorry if I've complained too much. I've just not traveled like this in a long time."

"No, don't apologize, Roxie." Lincoln rushed over to her and took her hands in his. "You haven't complained at all, really. You've been a trooper and you have nothing to apologize for. But give me ten minutes and I'll come right over, okay?"

"That sounds good." Roxie leaned over to peck a kiss on his cheek then went back to her bags to pull out a thin white cotton robe. It was enough to make her decent, but not too heavy.

"I'll be right back." Lincoln almost did a jig before he left the tent.

A few minutes later Lincoln came back with a pair of shorts and his tablet that he'd put on a solar charger earlier. "I have some movies downloaded on this thing, we can watch one if you want."

Once Lincoln had brought over a table to put his tablet on and changed into the much softer shorts he slept in, he sprayed their netting down with the bug repellent before he climbed into bed with her. "Want to cuddle or are you too hot?"

"I could use a cuddle I think." She replied with a pleased smile that she'd have hated two weeks ago. "I know it's silly, but I need to be near you."

"That's fine, Roxie. I don't mind at all." He pulled her into his arms, his skin as damp as hers from sweat but she didn't mind.

"I'll be okay tomorrow." She promised, her right cheek against his chest. "At least, I think I will."

Lincoln chuckled, making his chest rumble and even that was soothing, she was surprised to find. She never wanted to be vulnerable or needy, but at the moment, she was both. It was a good thing Lincoln was so kind and accepting.

"Are you happy I came with you?" She asked but cringed at how needy she sounded.

"I am, I think this will be a great experience for us both. You don't actually have to get involved, but we have a lot going on here. We've built a school already, and we have the team here teaching the villagers about cultivating the resources around them, though some of the older people are very wise in that regard and have taught us quite a lot too."

Roxie noted that hint of an English accent was becoming more pronounced as the minutes passed. He must be just as tired as she was, but it was nice talking with him like this. "Is there clean water, bathrooms? Things like that?"

"Yes, we've managed to get a clean water supply for them, they just have to maintain it. There's a lot of challenges to face here and between us all working together, we're trying to address those challenges."

"What kind of challenges? I thought Cambodia was a huge tourist spot?" Her left hand curled around his lower ribs and held him tight as she spoke.

"Not all of it." He answered softly, his voice getting quieter by the second. "There are a lot of rural villages here without much work for people. A lot of the men with families go off and work on farms in Thailand or anywhere they can find work. Unfortunately, some of those men come home with STDs from the women they sleep with while they're gone. Then their wives catch it and it can be a mess for them. There's also a lot of people that don't own land and well, let's talk more about it tomorrow. My brain is starting to shut down too."

He ended his summation with a self-conscious laugh that made her nudge at him with her knee. "Thank you,

I'll do some reading about the place when I can get a Wi-Fi signal."

"I know you will. The team here tells me there's a 4G carrier here, we'll get the SIM cards and all of that sorted tomorrow. What do you want to watch?" Lincoln listed off his movie collection and they settled on a classic mystery film.

It was one of the most romantic nights of her life, resting in that tent, sweating like mad, but feeling safe now that Lincoln was with her to scare away the boogie monsters. She smiled to herself as the film played on, Lincoln already snoring softly beside her in the cramped bed. No, there wasn't any sexy kind of stuff, but it was more like what she'd had with Nathan when they first started dating, something she hadn't realized she'd missed when he turned on her.

Just being with someone, sleeping like this, close to each other but nothing more, was what she'd thought marriage should be. Something like her parents' marriage, where you were comfortable being quiet and doing nothing with your partner. Which was a problem, as far as doing it with Lincoln was concerned, but it was only for a week or so. Surely, she'd get her fill of him in that time and she could put this all behind her when she got home?

For now, she just wanted to be beside him and enjoy the moment. She fell asleep before the film ended, but that was okay. They could always watch it another time.

* * *

THE NEXT DAY Roxie met up with Lincoln and the team for breakfast. She shared a secret smile with Lincoln. He'd slipped out of her tent at some point in the night because she woke up alone. That was fine, she didn't want to offend anyone any more than he did and now they had their own little secret between them. It was kind of…fun.

"Hey." She said as she came up beside him to get in line. "How did you sleep?"

"Like a baby until a mosquito got through the net and into my ankle. How are you?" He gave her a stroke across her cheek, a quick gesture to show her affection.

She'd have liked a kiss, but that would be far too overt, she figured.

"I'm good, feeling a little more rested. What are you going to be doing today?" She put fresh fruit and what turned out to be banana bread on her plate then they sat down on one of the benches set around long tables.

"I'll be viewing the damaged buildings up close and inspecting the new water treatment facility we set up. We want to build a better filter system for the village and find a way to use local products to do that. Industry is growing here but it's not keeping up and some of the team are working on using bamboo products as filters. It'll be a whole new industry that can provide income to the villagers."

"That sounds great," Roxie said once she'd swallowed some of the banana bread. "Want me to come with you?"

"You're still looking a little tired, Rox, why don't you stay here and get to know the locals?"

"I should be upset with you about that, but you're probably right. I am still a little tired and it would be nice to get to know some of the people here." She brushed her hair back from her face and tied it up, as it was looking a little cloudy outside and the wind had picked up. "Is it the rainy season here? I know some places over here have rain for months at a time, is this one of those places?"

"It can be yes. That's another problem with trying to build anything here, working around the rain." He sounded frustrated so she put a hand over his.

"You'll figure it out, Lincoln. I have faith in you. You've taken on something most rich men wouldn't think twice about. Not only that, but you are also hands-on about it, and that's impressive. I know you can overcome any challenges and you'll do it with the help of the people that live here." She really was impressed with what he was doing and wanted to praise him for it, even if he hadn't asked for it.

"Thanks, I have a good team and the locals are smart. They want to help and prosper here without having to migrate for work and struggle in the months when there is no work. A lot of them are migrant farmworkers, but I think I told you that last night." His cheeks turned pink again and Roxie felt herself smiling again.

"I remember you saying that. How about I sort out our phone stuff while you're gone?" She volunteered. She needed to text some of the people back home and she couldn't do that without any service here.

"Sure, I'll give you some money. They accept US dollars but don't be surprised if you get change back in riels."

"Riels?" Roxie asked blankly, but then she understood. "Oh, is that the local currency?"

"Yep, that's it. Okay, I'm going to meet up with Chris and get started. You be careful and have fun, okay?" He leaned over to peck her cheek, making her smile all over again.

"You too. I'll be around here somewhere when you finish." Roxie called out to him as he left.

The long trip had turned her into a gushy mess, she thought with a slight frown that didn't last long. It faded completely when she thought about that chaste kiss he'd given her. She was seeing a completely different side to Lincoln here than the one she saw back home. Here he was relaxed but vigilant, kind, generous, and charitable.

He'd given her $500 to play with and she wasn't even sure where to spend it yet.

Roxie sat in the covered area where all the volunteers, and some of the villagers, shared their meals. She was wondering what to do next. Where could she buy SIM cards and other stuff they might need? Roxie was about to get up and ask whoever she came to first, but she spotted Chantou heading towards the eating area. With a smile in place, Roxie walked up to the other woman.

"Hi, I was wondering if you could tell me where I can get a SIM card for my phone? Is there a shop nearby?"

"There's a place not far from here. I can show you if you like." Chantou offered and Roxie agreed.

"Let me just get my bag and I'll come right back," Roxie said and rushed off to get the backpack all her documents were in. It would be convenient for carrying back whatever she might buy.

"It's not a huge town, but it does have a few shops. It'll take about a half-hour to get there on this." They'd walked through the village until Chantou stopped in front of a blue Honda scooter.

"Hmm. Okay." Roxie had never been on one and it didn't look like it could hold both of them, but Chantou wouldn't have offered if she couldn't handle it. "That helmet for me?"

"Yes. If you haven't been on one of these before, my

advice is to lean into any turn, but not too much, and don't move around a lot on the back. Other than that, just enjoy being out in the fresh air." Chantou put on her own helmet, then backed the older model scooter up out of the area it was parked in.

"Cool. We can do this." Roxie got on when Chantou indicated she should, and they were soon speeding down a well-maintained dirt path.

For the first time since she'd left Myrtle Beach Roxie truly relaxed. Riding a scooter was much more fun than she'd ever imagined it could be.

15

Roxie

By the time she went back to her tent that night, the rain had started but at least she had service on her phone. The trip into the town, just a bigger village than the one they were in, showed Roxie that a lot of the houses were built of sturdy stuff, but there were quite a lot with thatching that some might call huts. All the buildings were on stilts in case of flooding.

Chantou had explained that most of the houses didn't have running water, which was why a well and filtration system were so necessary. Electricity was in short supply as well, but Lincoln's project had brought in solar panels for equipment and necessities. All of the people seemed happy enough, the women dressed in outfits that had matching tops and bottoms, all brightly colored and comfortable looking. Some women were in skirts while others wore pants. Long sleeves and short sleeves seemed to depend on the outfit, with many women wearing long sleeves despite the heat.

The town was comprised of sturdier buildings with terracotta roofs, and shelves crammed full of goods. By the time they returned to Chantou's village, Roxie's backpack was full of snacks, more mosquito repellent, and a few odds and ends she couldn't live without.

"Did you have a good day?" Lincoln interrupted her thoughts to ask as he came into her tent.

"Oh, it was really nice. Chantou took me into the town and when we came back, I spent time exploring the school with her and talking to the children. I love that school. Everyone seems so eager to teach or learn. And you give adult classes too, that's really wonderful." Roxie wanted to roll her eyes at herself, gushing all over him for the second time in less than 24 hours. But she was somehow a different person now, or maybe she was a different person *here*. She wasn't sure, but she kind of liked the person she felt she was here.

"You went to the school? That's great. It took us a while to find teachers that would stay put, but we have a great staff there now and a lot of my team members volunteer there too. It's one of the main things we try to do with the summer students that come here, get them involved in teaching the kids." Lincoln beamed with pride.

"It's amazing and I had no idea you'd done so much out here." Roxie moved over on the bed so he could sit down.

"You know, the only reason the floor hasn't turned to mud is we raised several areas around the village so they wouldn't flood. We plan to use the land the tents are on to build more housing for the people here. We have plans to put in more solar power and so much more. I think we could be here well beyond fifteen years."

Roxie found herself looking at Lincoln with admiration. This was not the guy she'd tried to avoid that night on the yacht or the guy she'd worked in an office with. This was a totally different Lincoln and, yeah, she admired him for it. "I'd really love to help out."

"You can have a week here with me, helping until your heart explodes with joy, my dear." He kissed the tip of her nose before he moved away.

"I know it's probably stupid, but helping at the school today, getting to know the kids, I really enjoyed that. "My efforts made the kids laugh, or helped them to understand and that's kind of how I felt working at Elmo's. What I did there was not the same at all, but on a micro-level, it was. I was teaching people what they wanted to know, helping them act out fantasies, their deepest, darkest desires that they wanted to explore, and

I loved that part more than anything. It's much nicer when it's kids learning English or how to add. It's a basic need, a basic right that all people should have, that basic need to understand how the world works. It's a basic human need that can be easily satisfied."

Lincoln didn't say anything, so she looked over at him. Maybe she'd made him mad with that comparison? The wonder on his face caught her by surprise. "What?"

"I think you've found a new calling, Princess Loly." He finally said after staring at her for a few more moments. "I like that."

"Don't call me that." She groused but it was a weak protest. She kind of liked how he said it now.

"Sorry, it's still a habit. Imagine not being able to say Chloe and calling yourself Loly." He smiled, reminding her of why she had the nickname.

In the past, it would have irritated her, him bringing up the past, but now? It wasn't so bad.

"Stop." She nudged him with her shoulder. "So, what's tomorrow bringing?"

"We're going to repair a roof on one of the houses we've already built." He started, but she interrupted him.

"Wait, you're actually going to carry wood up a ladder and get your own hands dirty?" She couldn't believe it. He had such well-manicured hands, smooth hands that didn't have calluses on them.

"I am, yes. Why? I'm not just a pretty face you know."

He pulled her close to whisper the words to her. "Although, your face is much prettier to look at than mine."

"That's debatable, Link." She got her own dig in by calling him the nickname he hated.

"You might get a spanking if you do that again." He growled along her throat and she had to hold back a loud giggle. They were still in the village, where anyone could hear what was going on in the tent.

"Don't you make promises you can't keep here." She turned to pull him down onto the bed with her while his hand reached out to turn off the lantern on the bedside table.

"I can keep some promises, Roxie." He whispered against her lips as heat flared to life between them.

"Then show me, Lincoln. Don't tell me, show me." She whispered back before she caught his lips with hers.

There was something different about the moment they shared this time. She'd always hated the term making love. It was fucking or sex to her but this? The soft, gentle way he touched her, the way they seemed to worship each other and merge in those dark hours they spent together, might just be making love. When it was over, they clung together, both too tired to speak.

Roxie turned, realizing they hadn't used a condom, but not caring. It was a safe time in her cycle, she hoped. She didn't want to get pregnant. Motherhood wasn't in the stars for her, but she enjoyed the special moment they shared and didn't want to spoil it with worry about pregnancies.

"Thank you for bringing me here, Lincoln. I think I needed it." She said finally, though she wasn't sure if he was still awake.

"It's my pleasure, Rox. Thanks for agreeing to come with me. I know we haven't spent much time together here, but we will at some point. And we have the nights to spend together. That makes this place even more special."

"I'm glad I came with you." Her fingers twined into his in the darkness and for a while, they were quiet, listening to the rain.

Roxie was glad the tent had a sturdy plastic floor, otherwise, she'd be walking around in mud. Whoever bought these tents knew what they were doing.

* * *

A COUPLE OF DAYS PASSED, and Lincoln said they'd have to stay a little while longer. The only problem was, he needed to go to Singapore to take care of some business there.

"Do you want to go with me and go back home?" He asked late in the evening.

"No. I'd like to stay another week, please? Pretty

please?" She balled her hands up under her chin and blinked her eyelashes at him with a grin. "I don't want to leave yet."

"If you're sure you want to stay, that's fine with me." He kissed the tip of her nose, a habit he had now, and went to sit in one of the camp chairs arranged around her tent. He still maintained his own tent, but he spent most of his evenings in here with her. "I don't want to fly out there, but it has to be done. I'd rather stay here with you though."

His eyes locked onto her and Roxie was shocked to read what he'd left unspoken written all over his face. *He'd love to stay here with her forever.* For a second, Roxie was sure her own face said the same thing, but she looked away.

Forever was a long time and they still had the contract, and, well, life was complicated. She didn't deserve, couldn't afford, to think about forever with anyone. She'd lost too much already. But maybe. Maybe she could pretend while she was here, that there was a chance for that.

They made love again that night, with him remembering the condom this time. It was slow, gentle, and brought out the stars and the sky behind her eyes. Slow and hushed, Lincoln claimed her in a way she'd never been claimed before. She was certain he'd consumed every part of her soul completely, with his slow caresses and the urging of his body.

When she woke up the next morning, she had a smile on her face even though she was alone in the narrow bed. It was as she taught a group of 7-year-olds how to say 'red' in English that she finally understood it wasn't just Lincoln that had caused this odd change in her thoughts and feelings, it was the people of this village that had changed her as well. It was a good change, she decided, a positive step forward that she wouldn't resist.

She remembered the last time Emily's mother had tried to insult her, how she'd sneered that Roxie's parents must be ever so proud of her, and couldn't help but hold her head up a little higher. Her parents would be proud if they knew who she was now, even with the stripping and pole dancing part of her life. She was a decent human being, at least, which was more than could be said for some people born with a silver spoon in their sour mouths.

Since the day she finally picked herself up out of the memory of the ashes of her burned-down home and the death of her parents, Roxie had not cowed before anyone. But being here taught her that she wasn't as bad as she thought she was. She'd had to work hard and fight to be where she was back home, but here? Here she got the chance to be so much more than she ever thought she'd get a chance to be.

Lincoln had promised that he'd only be gone for a day or two and two days had passed without him coming back. She wasn't surprised to know she missed him and wanted him to come back to the village. It might have been easier if he'd been able to call her or text, but he must have been really busy because there was no contact from him at all.

The hours passed though, filled with teaching kids dance moves after school and playing with them. She made more friends, both with the team working there and the locals. For a while, she actually felt like a necessary part of a community and it was…nice.

In the evenings she talked with Wendy through video chats, she called Emily once, and texted the girls she used to work with. They were all really excited to hear about what Roxie was doing in Cambodia and it felt good to have their support. But then, she'd always had the support of her friends, she just hadn't been in the habit of accepting it too often. Maybe that would change when she went back home.

When Roxie woke up on the third morning of Lincoln's absence, she headed over to the eating area to get breakfast. The sky was dark and ominous, so it wasn't a surprise when she heard the others talking about a storm that was supposed to arrive in three days. Roxie didn't say anything to anyone but if they'd asked her opinion, she'd have told them that storm was arriving early.

She spent the day helping the adult villagers with their English pronunciation and was about to go to lunch when the wind picked up drastically. She could see why Lincoln was so eager to get the buildings repaired here in the village. The repairs had continued while he was gone and most of them were done now, with the help of so many people. It looked like they'd finished just in time for another storm to tear through.

Thunder started to echo through the long row of houses in the village, houses that looked like something out of the *Three Little Pigs* story, while Roxie wandered back to her tent. When rain started to pour down on the tent in a heavy torrent and the wind threatened to pull it up out of the ground, Roxie gathered up her things and went over to the temporary community center. It was the sturdiest building there.

She wasn't the only one who had that idea because she saw almost the entire village and Lincoln's crew sitting on chairs and the floor, waiting to ride out the storm. The downpour only grew worse, threatening even the sturdiest buildings in the village. The door to the community center flung open and everyone gasped, their heads turning to the door.

"Sorry, folks, I got here a little late. That's a nasty storm out there." Lincoln strode into the room and went straight for Roxie, pulling her into his arms despite the fact that his clothes were soaked. "Fuck, I missed you."

He whispered the words against her ear and she took them into her heart with a thrill she'd never felt before. Not even those love letters she'd exchanged with Liam, his half-brother, all those years ago had thrilled her as much as Lincoln's words did now.

"I missed you too. Want to sit with me?" She indicated her small pile of belongings and he took a seat with her.

One of the men from his team came over with a couple of towels and Lincoln did his best to dry off but it didn't help much. He had a small backpack that held clothes but the rain had gotten into that too. She was about to offer him one of the extra blankets she'd brought when she heard the sound of a car horn going off and a deep thudding followed by the sound of metal screaming.

"What the fuck was that?" Lincoln jolted up and ran out of the door before she could stop him. The storm was getting worse and something terrible had just happened. Roxie got up and followed him out the door without a second thought.

16

Lincoln

*L*incoln wasn't sure what he saw when he ran out of the door, it was dark and there was only a single beam of light shining out of the darkness. He rushed towards the light, trying to figure out what happened. It was obviously the horn of an automobile that was still going off, but what had happened?

The situation became obvious when he drew closer and saw the front of a bus wrapped around a tall palm tree. The tree had snapped at the top and blocked the road now.

The sound of the horn stopped, and the sliding door of the bus opened. A short man with black hair and tanned skin stepped down, looking dazed. "What happened?"

"I think you hit the tree. Follow that lady inside, she'll get you help." Lincoln directed in English since the man had spoken English. "Roxie, take him inside please, and don't come back out. It's too dangerous out here for you."

"I will, Lincoln." She agreed, and he was glad for it. He didn't want to argue about how she was grown and could do what she wanted to. He simply wanted to find out if there were more people on the bus and get them out.

With a swipe of his face to clear water from his eyes, Lincoln climbed aboard to find far more people than expected. "Hi, do any of you speak English?"

"I'm here, Lincoln." A woman announced and when she stood up Lincoln understood. The woman was named Dara and she was from the next village.

"What are you doing here, Dara? Are any of you hurt?" He asked once she got closer to him.

"Our shelter collapsed, and we wanted to come here. I think one of the tires blew out and we hit that tree." She pointed at the front of the bus and put a swatch of cloth under her nose when it started to bleed. "I'm fine, just a busted nose. It's the other bus I'm worried about. It's not arrived yet."

"Okay, if you can help me to get these people off the

bus," Lincoln said, looking at the pain-filled faces of a busload of elderly people.

He wasn't sure who was hurt and who was just suffering from old age but he started to carry people out, male or female, and took them into the clinic area of the center. A nurse was there, checking over the bus driver and then each new person he brought in. Some of the other men from the village and his team helped to get more people off as the minutes ticked away.

Should he go out in this weather to see what had happened to the other bus? There were still people on this bus that needed help getting off, over forty of them, if he'd counted correctly. It had been packed when he first got to the bus, but it wasn't as bad now. He was soaking wet again but didn't notice it until he picked someone up and they cringed at how cold his body had become, despite his exertions. His hair was plastered to his head and he was growing more tired with each person he carried in.

Every now and then he saw Roxie's face pop up to check on him, but she didn't get in his way. He wanted her to stay inside, where it was safe, so he didn't ask her to help. He'd spent the last three days without her and he'd been nothing but miserable the entire time. He'd wanted to spend the night holding her. He'd raced to get there before the storm got too bad and this accident was a perfect example of why it wouldn't be good to be on the roads right now.

They'd just have to wait to see if the other bus showed up with the younger people and their families. Lincoln continued to ferry people off the bus. He paused on the way back to the bus to check whether anyone was left. He could hear the sounds of cows calling out in the darkness and the water buffalo that usually wandered around in the rice patties when they weren't being used to plow. The animals would ride out the storm fine, it was the people that were in danger for now.

He thought again about that other bus, wondering how much time had passed and what it meant that the bus hadn't arrived. He knew Cambodia was trying to grow its economy and the loss of so many young people could really hurt the village they were from. The elderly couldn't provide food and money for themselves and they might starve to death in the lean times, if not for the younger generation sending money back home when they went off to work in other places.

He saw the bus was empty when he jogged back up the steps and took a look around. He wanted to be sure one of the elderly people hadn't slipped in their seat, asleep or too injured to cry out for help. He was about to turn around to get off the bus when two bright lights blinded him. He waved, knowing that the driver probably couldn't see him, but felt relief that the other bus had arrived at last.

That relief turned to fear that plunged his heart down into his stomach when the lights grew brighter as they drew closer. "Fuuuuuuck."

That was about all he had to say as the lights glowed even brighter and then he was thrown against a seat. He grabbed the back of the seat but lost his grip when the bus flipped over onto its side. The sound of shattered glass and shrieking metal overrode the sound of the rain and thunder as the world went dark around him.

Lincoln's body thudded onto the roof. His head hit pretty hard as he fell and it felt like his face ripped away as his cheek slid across cold metal. He tasted blood in his mouth and was about to yell when hand luggage, shopping bags full of household items, and the rest of the things the villagers had brought with them started to rain down on him.

"Fucking hell, are you fucking serious?" He curled into a tight ball and wondered if this prolonged nightmare was ever going to end.

Everything went quiet after that. He took a deep breath, did a mental inspection of his body, and was thankful it was only his head and his face that hurt. He pushed luggage off himself, gazed at a very peed-off chicken in a cage, and reached up his hand to feel his face. Friction burn on his face, he decided when he felt no tears or cuts, and a nasty knot on his head, but it wasn't bleeding. He'd live.

It was a struggle to get up but he managed it and looked at the windows beside him. Worrying he might be about to break his legs or slice them open on glass, Lincoln ignored the worries and settled down on the inside roof of the bus to kick out the glass panel nearest him. The emergency door latch was too high up for him to reach, and the back end of the bus was filled with the front end of the other bus. How the driver hadn't seen the downed tree or the stopped bus was beyond him, but it was obvious the man had driven right into the first bus.

He struggled to get out, but finally, he did. Oddly, it was that moment when everything became super loud. Or maybe his ears had just decided to work again. He could hear Roxie screaming his name on the outside of the bus, her voice not the only one calling out in the darkness.

"Roxie. Babe. I'm fine!" He called out to her. He smiled when he saw her turn with a tear-streaked face, his heart clenching in his chest at her expression filled with hope. "I'm fine, princess. I really am."

She rushed to him and wrapped her arms around his waist, her face pressed into somewhere around his ribs. "Oh, thank fuck for that. Fucking hell, that bus plowed right into you while I was standing there watching. I thought I'd died just then."

"It's alright, princess, I'm here." He held her tight as the other men patted him on the back on the way to the other bus. That required some getting into because the front had smashed so far in, the door was nonexistent now. Some of the quick thinkers in the village started to bring over ladders and they climbed up to help the families off. "I'm going to help them, Roxie, and after that, I'm not moving from your side for the rest of the night. Go on now, go inside, you're shivering and soaking wet."

It was still raining but Lincoln didn't care. He had to help get those kids out. The men formed a chain, one in the bus handing down babies that were passed down a line of men until they reached Lincoln who carried them to the villagers still inside the center. He saw Roxie, staring at him with pure admiration and almost blushed except he was too damn cold. He went back out for another baby, this one followed by her mother, and then more.

In total there were 27 babies, 33 children under ten, and twenty younger adults on the bus. Younger in comparison to the old people Lincoln had helped off the other bus. By the time they'd finished clearing the bus, everyone was saved except the driver. He hadn't survived the impact and was crushed by the weight of the engine. That cast a deeper pallor over the evening that couldn't be brightened even when he sank down into Roxie's arms.

They'd worked hard to keep most public displays of affection to a minimum, but he didn't care right now. He just wanted to inhale her scent and feel the soft skin on the inside of her wrist until his body stopped aching. He kissed her neck quietly, quickly, and sighed in happiness.

Roxie wasn't having any of his polite cuddles at all. She tilted his face up to hers, kissed him passionately, and ignored the giggles of the teenage girls in the room. The kiss brought him back to life in a way that was not conducive to being in public and he pulled away. "Later. When we can go back to your tent, I'll ravish you to within an inch of your life, but not right now, babe."

"Ravish me? Oh, indeed." Her eyebrow perked up and she laughed a soft, dirty laugh that made him twitch all over in need.

"Don't make this harder on me." He implored her, but that only earned him another one of those throaty chuckles.

"And how hard is it, Lincoln? Is it throbbing and hot, or solid and aching?" She whispered that into his ears and this time he did feel the heat in his cheeks.

"Both, you little tease. That's it, you're Princess Lolita from now on." He whispered back and felt her move in surprise.

"Princess Lolita? Why?" She seemed curious, as he knew she would be.

"Because you've tortured me since you were a teenager with your gorgeous eyes and sultry lips that beg to be crushed in hot kisses. Because I want to drag you out of here like the tease you are and fuck the tease out of you."

"Oh. Oh my." Hers were the cheeks that turned red this time.

Lincoln smiled in satisfaction. He'd shut her up, at least.

* * *

FOUR HOURS later they were warm, dry, and snuggled up in Roxie's tiny bed. Her naked body was warm and comforting against his, soothing away the soreness that was starting to form in his joints. "Well, at least I can say I know exactly what it feels like to be hit by a bus and mean it."

"Oh, that's not funny, Lincoln." Roxie protested but she kissed his neck right under the side of his jawline.

"No, but it is if you're the one that got hit by a bus. While on a bus." He laughed softly, his body starting to respond to the intimate touch of her hands over his skin. "Mmm, that feels good."

"I should hope so. You should just be happy you can

feel anything. After getting hit by a bus." She let out a quiet giggle and scrunched up in his arms when he dug a finger into her waist.

"Don't take the piss." He replied with one of his British sayings that always made her eyebrows rise up on her forehead. This time it only made her laugh.

"Just be glad you can still piss." She started, but he finished it.

"After getting hit by a bus? Yes, I suppose I should be." He laughed with her before he pulled her tightly. "But I promised you a spanking after."

"Maybe I don't want to be spanked. Maybe I want more of what you gave to me a few nights ago." She looked straight into his eyes, inviting far more intimacy than a mere fuck would give them.

"But I thought you didn't like vanilla sex. Wasn't it too boring for you?" He asked the question meaning to continue the teasing game they'd started, but the game had suddenly turned serious.

"Not with you, Lincoln. It's never been boring with you." Her tense eyes told him she felt vulnerable and was probably holding far more back than she let on.

"Are you sure, Roxie? I don't want you to do something you don't want to do." Like get attached, then leave him again, or worse, let him get attached and then leave him again.

"I'm sure, Lincoln. I like what you've taught me."

Roxie said with an easy wink. "It's been enlightening, being here with you."

"I see." He answered, but he wasn't sure he did. What did that imply about their relationship? Would it turn into an actual relationship now or would it continue as a contract? He'd already decided he wanted to extend the contract, if she insisted on keeping it, for far longer than they'd initially planned. But would she accept an offer for more than that from him?

17

Roxie

Lincoln kissed her deeply, softer than he'd ever kissed her before, but with so much intensity it nearly took her breath away. Roxie brought her hands up to his face, to touch him, feel him, and make sure this was all real. Cambodia had brought her many things, but for the first time since the night of the fire ten years ago, she felt like she could be herself.

Nobody here knew her past, apart from Lincoln, or knew who she was before she came here. There was no judgment, no need to hide and she felt free here. She felt freer than she ever had before and that was what made this place really special. Lincoln had brought her here and he'd given her a bigger gift than an exotic vacation. He'd given her the freedom to breathe in peace.

Her lips moved with his as he traced her tongue with his. Having him over her, cradled in her thighs, so intimately pressed into her, made her aware suddenly of just how different this was with him here. Back home, they both stood aloof from each other, sparring for the dominant position, but here? They were two people sharing something far more than pleasure.

A tear formed in her eye and she pulled away from him, caught up in something she didn't want to define yet.

"What's wrong?" He asked quietly, his eyes seeking through the darkness, spearing into her to find what had made her pull back.

"I'm just overwhelmed from the accident I guess." She dismissed the moment, a smile back in place. "Kiss me again, Lincoln."

She moved back to him but instead of kissing her, he…hugged her.

She'd been hugged a million times in her life. By her parents, friends, lovers along the way. She'd hugged strangers and acquaintances and knew what it felt like. Sometimes it felt awkward, or good. Sometimes it even felt soothing. This hug, however, felt like a place she'd been missing had finally been found.

Calm took over, wiped gently at the overwhelming thing that had nearly brought her to tears, and soothed her once more. Her body relaxed in Lincoln's arms, allowed her to enjoy his touch in ways she never had before. As a partner.

"I'm fine now, Lincoln. I promise." She finally whispered to him, but he continued to hold her.

She'd been a teen on the run the first time she'd slept with him, the first time she'd slept with any man. Now, she was a grown woman, who had nothing to fear, for the moment at least. She could relax. She could enjoy what Lincoln gave her. She could enjoy being *alive* for the first time that she could remember.

"Lincoln." She pulled away to look at him, a smile on her face. "Kiss me?"

"As you please, Princess Lolita." He murmured against her jawline before his lips moved up to hers.

The kiss lasted for days, or so it seemed. Her body moved against his as the kiss lingered, wanting more, wanting to be touched. Her hands clutched at his strong swimmer's shoulders, slid down his narrow waist with pure enjoyment at how well-made he was, before cupping over the round tense muscles of his ass. He had a perfect ass to dig her nails into.

No matter that she needed a manicure after digging around in the dirt with the kids when they played, or when the adults planted new vegetables. It didn't matter that her hands were no longer smooth but covered in nicks from cutting down vegetation with the women as they cleared land for a new building. None of it mattered when she pushed at his ass to tilt his hips deeper into hers.

All that mattered was how he groaned into her mouth, how his hips pressed his hard length into the heat of her center. Lincoln moved down her body, worshiping her neck, her collar bone, before moving down to tease a nipple into a tight peak with the heated confines of his mouth. His lips sucked at the peak, his tongue darting at it in time with the hand that slid down between her thighs.

He let the nipple go, only to capture the other and torture it with his sensual attention. Roxie enjoyed having her nipples teased, enjoyed it a lot, but Lincoln rarely used his mouth on them when they were back home. Here, they had none of the toys, the enhancements, that made sex a thrill. Here, they only had each other and what they were born with as their tools. It was almost primitive, but at the same time, she liked that very much.

It was something else that set them free as far as Roxie was concerned. Her hands began to move on him, to tease at his nipples while her mouth bit at the back of his neck where she could reach. He hissed in a breath when her teeth closed on his skin, and she bit a fraction harder. Her hands moved lower, to grasp at his cock, to tease the hard flesh while her teeth sank a little deeper.

"Fuck, that's good," Lincoln rasped, his hips pushing

into her hand, his head up, to allow her the access she needed to bite his neck. "Harder."

She smiled around his skin and bit just a little bit harder. Not enough to draw blood but enough that he could feel it, could feel the shimmer of pain that morphed into a very satisfying pleasure. She knew that sensation well and knew Lincoln enjoyed it as much as she did.

"Don't make me come yet, Roxie. Please." He begged her, admitting far more than he probably should have.

He was already about to burst, and that gave her power, even though this wasn't a power play. It did tell her that she had to go gently though, and she eased off a little. He wanted to last, wanted to make this last longer. They had all night as far as she was concerned.

His lips found their way to a nipple again and Roxie relaxed, letting him have his way. She didn't think about how she'd shied away from the intimacy of the moment when it became almost unbearable how much she felt for him. She didn't examine how she'd tried to make this sex again when he was offering her so much more. She just…gave in.

She let the fear that this might turn into something more go and allowed herself to truly feel what Lincoln made her feel. His hand left her inner thighs and moved around to her hip, to nudge her up into his. Her legs automatically went around his waist, wrapping him in her body.

She felt his length slide between her folds as she adjusted her body to cradle him more comfortably. It felt good and she wanted more. Their bodies started to move together, an imitation of the act they both wanted, but not yet. The hand on her hip moved further down as his face came back up to hers to kiss her with a need that nearly consumed them both.

Emotions threatened to overwhelm her again, but she didn't pull away, she let herself feel them. Those emotions were spurred on by the sounds Lincoln made, the gasps, the groans, the guttural growls when he broke the kiss for a moment of air. Roxie was adrift in a sea of things she couldn't define. Her body knew what they were though and carried her through them, keeping her afloat as her hands clutched at the back of his hair.

The hate she'd always swore she'd felt for him disappeared entirely as the heat between them consumed everything but her ability to want him and only him. That was also new, but she didn't mind at the moment. If one man could make her feel like this, she didn't need anyone else. It was that simple.

"Love me, Lincoln. Please?" She whispered, not afraid to ask for what she truly wanted, even if she didn't want to examine what she truly meant by love.

"Anything your heart desires, Princess." He whispered back just before he shifted between her thighs. In an instant, he was inside of her, deep inside her.

Only he didn't stop to adjust to the sensation of her body wrapped around his, he didn't pause to catch his breath, he just plunged into her, stealing every last thought from her mind and replacing it with him.

Her nails dug into his shoulders, claiming him as her own, prodding him to go deeper, to take more of her, all of her.

"Lincoln." She gasped his name against his neck, but he moved away, sitting up to pull her hips up to his, to hit just the right spot inside her. Roxie threw her arms over her head, gave herself up to him as his hands kneaded at her ass, provoking little shivers of pleasure from that part of her as well.

She held herself still as he thrust into her with concerted effort, his eyes on hers. She smiled up at him and he grinned back. But then a flutter started within her body, a flutter that turned into a pulse as their eyes remained locked together. Her mouth fell open in a gasp of surprise, her eyes determined to stay open as he sent her over the edge. But they closed, her hands grasping at his wrists as the pulse turned into a wave that took her far away from the world around her.

Pleasure pulsed into life, stole her thoughts and her voice. All she could do was sigh, then moan as her body drew taut as a bowstring and spasmed with each bolt of pleasure he pushed into her.

She thought she heard him gasp her name. Thought she heard a groan, but it didn't matter. Not when she was wrapped around him, was pulling him along with her until she felt a different sensation, a pulse that was not her own body, but his, as he finally lost control. She heard her name as a groan now, as a plea to take him to wherever she'd left him to go.

It was the sweetest thing she'd ever heard and she wanted to hear it again, for the rest of her life.

But she didn't have time to think too much about it, not when the flutters started again, not when he continued to stroke into her, pulling another torrent of pleasure from her one more time.

When it was finished, when there was nothing more to do but catch their breath and stroke each other. Roxie listened to the night around them. She didn't want to think, refused to think, so she listened to the sounds of Lincoln's breath, to the pulse of his blood in his veins that slowly calmed down. She heard animals out in the fields beyond the village, the cry of a baby that wanted its mother.

She took it all in, stamping it into her memory so that she could pull it out later. There were things she'd missed, things she'd ignored, but she'd felt those things. She'd lived those things and later when she was alone, she'd face the things she didn't want to admit. But now. For now, she just wanted to feel, to be free to feel, and so she did.

Lincoln withdrew from her, rolled onto his side, and tucked her up against his body. Their skin began to cool, and the race of their hearts slowed down. Roxie listened as Lincoln whispered to her softly, telling her something, but she was losing the fight to stay awake. She thought he was talking about making a life here with her, in a rectangular hut of their own, about how he wanted her to have his children, be his wife, and live a life of peace in Cambodia. But maybe it was all a dream.

She woke up a few hours later, felt him hard against her hip, heard his gentle snores, and knew he was asleep. Her hands moved of their own will, took him in a grip that didn't wake him, but moved still the same. She listened in the darkness, heard the moment his body became aware it was being touched so intimately.

Her hand stroked and pulled at him and she moved in the darkness. He didn't wake, his body remained relaxed, but when her lips wrapped around him, she felt his legs go tight, and heard a gasp of surprised pleasure. His hands came down to her hair and guided her movements. She nudged him with her free hand and he moved flat to his back as she climbed between his legs.

The free hand then moved between her own legs as she pleasured him with her mouth. Every pulse of his cock in her mouth, every gasp of his pleasure only enhanced her own excitement. Giving him this pleasure did not feel subservient, not when she got so much pleasure out of doing it.

She increased her pace, working him with her mouth and a hand, all while pleasuring herself as well, until she heard his breath catch in his throat, felt his body go rigid. The spot where her finger worked between her thighs sparked to life, and she moaned around him as he pulsed into her mouth. The control it took not to bite him only enhanced the pleasure, directed it down to her clit as Lincoln groaned her name and emptied into her mouth.

The pleasure ended on a sigh from Lincoln as she pulled her mouth away from him and pushed up to lie beside him. He took her in his arms, and they fell asleep together again. But she heard him whisper a thank you just before sleep took her. She didn't know it, but she smiled throughout her sleep this time.

When she woke up, Lincoln was still in bed with her. She examined his face, saw how the tension that was ever-present had disappeared. She saw him truly relaxed and wanted more of that. Her fingers came up, traced the outline of his dark eyebrow, trailed down his face to trace his jaw. His eyelids opened and dark brown orbs crashed into blue.

"Good morning." He said with a smile. "Seems I didn't sneak back to my own tent last night."

"I think it's okay, all the women seem to know something is going on. They call you my man." She replied with a soft smile, scrubbing at her own face to remove any traces of sleep that might linger.

"Well then, I guess we're alright then." His eyes narrowed, examining her. "Are you alright? You seem…different."

"I'm fine, really, Lincoln. Just…" She paused, rolled her eyes up as if thinking, and then spoke again. "Happy I think."

"Ah, that's good then, right?" He pulled her hips to his and kissed her.

"It is. And I'd like nothing more than to spend the day here in this tiny bed with you, but I'm hungry and need a shower desperately." She grinned before she got up to climb over him. "Come on, we have stuff to do."

"Yes, ma'am." He moaned but didn't make a move to get out of bed.

"Come on then." She turned to face him as she pulled a t-shirt over her head and slid on a pair of shorts. "Maybe you can sneak into the shower room with me."

That got him to move and she left the tent with a laugh of happiness. She was in such a good mood she didn't even think to remind him of how much she hated him.

18

Roxie

The horror and desperation she'd felt as she watched that bus ram into the other bus replayed itself in Roxie's mind over the next week. She had been able to ignore the panic and terror she felt that first night, but since then, it replayed itself when she least expected it. She didn't like it one bit that she suddenly had a need to know where he was at all times, as if afraid he'd disappear if she couldn't keep her eyes on him.

Otherwise, she was happier than she'd been in a long time. They stayed in Cambodia to help the other village get back on its feet and spent their nights together. Roxie didn't cringe anymore when she thought the words 'making love', she only smiled brighter. That's what they were doing, making love, not fucking as they'd done before.

Lincoln worked with the men during the day, and she worked at the school or outside with the women. They'd share smiles as they passed each other, traded kisses in dark corners of buildings at lunchtime, held hands under the table whenever they ate, and generally acted like teenagers who'd just discovered what it was like to have a crush.

Roxie had never seen Lincoln smile so much. He was a natural frowner, worrying over something at all times. But as the days passed in their peaceful hideaway, the frown disappeared, smoothed into a look of contentment. They both worked hard, saw the evidence of their efforts, and that added to the feeling of contentment she hadn't expected at all.

There were a lot of things she hadn't expected, like how nice it was to watch Lincoln, shirt off, working on a roof. It nearly made her growl with pride that he looked so damn good using his body for physical work. She hadn't been very discreet when she'd growled and Chantou nearly fell down laughing at Roxie's reaction.

"You're like a woman that's been locked away from a man for far too long." Chantou laughed, but spoke quietly, so as not to further embarrass Roxie. "You growl like tiger, ready to pounce."

Roxie's face had gone red, and she glared at the woman when she made a biting motion with her teeth and held up her hands in claws. "You're a terrible person, Chantou. I can't help it."

Chantou's face fell and Roxie rushed to reassure her that she'd only been joking. "No, don't stop, I know you're only teasing. I'm sorry, my friend."

So she also learned about being gentle with people that didn't speak English as their first language and came from a different culture. She'd learned so much on this trip and she really should thank Lincoln for inviting her to come along.

"Do you love him?" Chantou asked her now, as they stared at Lincoln and some of the men trekking out into the forest to collect bamboo.

"No!" Roxie protested instantly, her brows furrowed, and her lips pursed. "I don't do love."

"I don't understand, what does this mean? 'You don't do love'?" Chantou sat up on the bench, her arms crossed under her breasts. "This makes no sense to me."

"It means I don't have time to fall in love. Back home I take care of myself, I work hard, and well, there's things I don't talk about. Love just isn't for me." She spoke the words, but her own heart and Chantou's face declared the statements bullshit.

"I see how you look at him, Roxie. You like him." She nodded to affirm her own thoughts, her frown deepening. "Denying you love him will only hurt you both in the long run, you know?"

"It's impossible to love him, Chantou. I've only been with him a few weeks." Which brought to life the fact that their contract was almost up. That wasn't the topic of the moment, however. "Okay, I've known him my whole life, more or less, but still. Lincoln is just my…"

"Love?" Chantou did an imitation of Roxie's own lifted-eyebrow look, her eyes stubbornly declaring Roxie was lying to herself.

"No. I'm crazy about him, okay, I'll give you that, but it's not love. It can't be."

"I know, I know, you don't do love. Whatever you say, my friend." Chantou patted Roxie's arm and smiled a knowing smile before she looked away. "He doesn't 'do' love either, I guess?"

"No, I don't think he does." Roxie ignored the hint of sadness in her voice. "I have to get back to the kids, I'll talk to you later, Chantou."

"See you, my friend." Chantou waved her off but Roxie could still feel her friend's eyes on her as she walked away.

How could she explain something she didn't understand herself?

She loved the way Lincoln made her feel. She loved the way he called her Princess Lolita when they were alone, shortening it to Loly when they were in public and he wanted to goad her. She loved how he was generous, kind, and hardworking too. She loved how they laughed together, how they worked together. There were countless things she loved about him, but that didn't mean she actually *loved* him, did it?

Roxie's last day in the village passed quickly, with a dinner in the communal eating area and a goodbye from all the children before she and Lincoln boarded a bus to take them back to a hotel in Phnom Penh. Roxie was sad to leave her new friends behind, but Lincoln had already planned a trip back in the less rainy season. She was quiet as they left the bus and walked into the hotel late that evening.

"You okay, Loly?" He asked, his head bent towards her, their hands clasped as they rode up in the elevator.

"I'm fine, just a little sad, that's all. I'll miss them all so much."

"That's always the hard part, leaving them all behind. The havoc of the next few days as we head home doesn't compare to how hard it is to leave the village sometimes." He brought her hand up to his mouth to kiss it just before the doors opened and they went to their room.

Roxie took a shower, put on a thin nightgown, and sat down in an armchair to stare out at the city below.

She'd been so exhausted when she was here last time that she hadn't truly taken in how huge the city was. Bright lights from buildings and cars lit up the night and the noise reached them, even up here on the third floor. She felt like she'd been dumped into a new world, a world she understood but no longer wanted to live in. It was a struggle not to beg Lincoln to take her back to the village, to leave her there if he absolutely had to go back.

She didn't realize she was crying until he knelt in front of her and drew her into his arms. She sank into his arms and sobbed in a way she hadn't done since that first night she'd spent with him when they were both so young and afraid.

He'd been able to go on and live his life, but she'd had to hide who she was, become someone new. She'd become so different from the girl she used to be that she barely recognized that girl anymore. But in that village, she'd almost remembered who she was, almost remembered the hopes and dreams she'd put away so that she could take care of herself. Lincoln held her, making soothing sounds that didn't demand she speak the pain she felt, and she was grateful for that.

"It's been hard on you." He said when the sobs calmed to sniffles. He sat back on his feet and looked up at her. "Not life in the village, but being on your own."

"Yeah, it has." She admitted with a watery smile.

"That's why I loved being in the village so much, I think. I didn't have to pretend to be anything. I didn't have to work at watching my back, or always be careful not to give away who I am."

"But you are that person, Rox." He said it softly, broaching something he knew she didn't want to.

"I know, Lincoln, but let's not talk about that right now, please? Let me just be your Loly for now, okay? I like being Loly." She smiled and wiped at her face with a towel he handed to her.

"I can do that." He got up to go to the bar fridge, took out two small bottles of bourbon and a can of Coca-Cola. "Here, have a drink with me."

He mixed the contents of the bottles and the can in two glasses on a tray and brought them to her. "Cheers."

"Yeah, thanks." She took the drink and sipped it, her eyes back on the city outside. "I guess I need to stop whining and get ready for the hell you're about to put me through over the next few days."

"It's not something I look forward to either, but we can do it." He sipped at his drink and sat back in the chair opposite hers. "What are you going to do when we get back?"

"Sleep. For a week." She looked down at her chipped and pitted nails and frowned. "And get a manicure."

"Mm, there's the Roxie I know." He grinned at her

and looked away. "I need a haircut and a week of sleep myself."

"We're a pair, aren't we?" She snickered and sipped her drink.

"It seems so, yes." He replied softly. "But, I'm going to shower now and get to bed."

He put his empty glass on the table and looked at her. "Care to join me?"

"I think I'll finish my drink and see what's on TV." She looked at the bed, almost too big for them, and missed her tiny bed in the village. "I'll be waiting for you, though."

"Alright." Lincoln nodded and went into the bathroom.

She was a little embarrassed that she'd lost control like that, and a little ashamed that she'd cried. She needed a moment to regain her equilibrium, but something told her that wouldn't happen until she was back home and into the swing of her old life. She didn't want to think about that, about how easy it would be to slip back into her old self.

For a little while longer, she wanted to retain the person she'd been in that village. A person that had hope, who was carefree and laughed easily. There was no doubt in her mind that the minute she stepped back onto American soil she'd have to start looking over her shoulder. Since her parents had died she'd done that every single day.

She'd never known quite what happened, but she'd put together the knowledge that those men had beat up her dad and were there the night of the fire. That meant the fire hadn't been an accident. There'd always been the question of whether her father set the fire or those men, but to Roxie the answer was obvious, those men had meant to kill her parents. The reason she always looked over her shoulder was clear; they'd meant to kill her as well. Since they hadn't accomplished that, she assumed she was a target and had hidden who she used to be, who she was now, with great care.

Until Lincoln came along, that is.

The problem was compounded by the fact that Lincoln's family would recognize her. His mother, his siblings, all of them would know who she was. Which meant she couldn't have a real relationship with him.

She smiled, thinking of her teenage crush on his half-brother Liam. She still had one of his letters, hidden away back at her apartment. They'd exchanged those letters, hidden in a birdhouse, for months. Strange how it was Lincoln that she'd ended up sleeping with, losing her virginity to him that awful night. How it was Lincoln she was with now.

He came out of the shower, his hips wrapped in a towel,

and she held her arms out to him, needing his strength the moment she saw him. He didn't say anything, didn't ask anything, he just came to her and gave her what she needed. She didn't speak either, she just took what he offered her and drank in his attention. Maybe even his love.

But she knew he didn't believe in love. She wasn't so sure she did either, but her memory always prodded her with images of her parents, how they looked at each other, and always found ways to touch. Was that love? She wondered as he took her breath away, his mouth intimately pressed into her center. Was this need to always be near him, love?

It couldn't be, but she wished it was as her brain exploded with the many hues of pleasure he worked to give her. He was a magnificent man, even if he could be an asshole when he wanted to be. If only he could keep his mouth shut about who she was, keep her secret for her, they might be able to make this something more than a contract.

If he could keep her secret then she wouldn't turn down whatever came next. Their contract was almost over. Somewhere during the hectic hours of getting back to Myrtle Beach, the contract would end. What came next was up to Lincoln.

If he wanted to keep her in his life, he'd do what needed to be done. He'd respect her need for privacy, secrecy, and make sure he protected her at all times. The way he sank into her with a sigh of pure bliss told her he would do just that. What man could turn away from someone who made him feel like that?

She held him close, urged him on, hoping that whatever came next, whatever happened to her, that she could hold him like this for a little while longer. For only a little while longer.

19

Lincoln

Conflict in his personal life was something Lincoln had always hated. If that conflict came from his business dealings he'd relish the fight, do whatever it took to win, but in his personal life? No, he only wanted peace there. Which was one reason he didn't mind moving so far away from his mother and siblings.

His mother could never settle with one man, showing him that love was not real between spouses. She'd changed marriages and homes like other women changed clothes, without regret and no looking back. After her divorce from Dr. Bennet all those years ago, he'd stopped getting to know her new men. They never lasted and walking away from a father figure was a hard thing to do.

He understood his real father had been a bastard to her, and he suspected her own mother had taught her some hard lessons about life, but he'd only ever wanted a steady, peaceful home. He'd almost started to think he could have that here in Myrtle Beach, away from the hectic life in New York City, away from his family.

Life with Roxie in Cambodia had been the most peaceful time in his life. Sure, he'd been literally hit by a bus, and there'd been the quick trip to Singapore, but the nights with her had been…perfect.

Three days had passed since they'd made it back to their real lives and he'd had a lot of time to think. She'd rested the first couple of days but had sent him a text earlier today saying she was going out with Emily to get her nails done and have lunch. He'd smiled at the kiss emoji she sent along with the text, remembering that night in the village when she woke him with her mouth wrapped around him.

His body responded immediately, but he ignored it. He had a lot to do, a lot to sort through since he'd been gone for two weeks, not the few days he'd planned. Yeah, he loved being with her, loved how close they were, but it was a weakness he couldn't afford right now. He had to watch over her, make sure he found out who the bastards were that were after her in the past, and protect her from the new threats that asshole Nathan had brought to her.

Nathan was still in hiding. Tanya and Kai were working with the security team to try to trace him and the new guys that were after Nathan and Roxie both. Lincoln was considering contacting one of his oldest friends, a man who'd dropped off the radar lately. A man that was entrenched in the Italian Mafia from the moment he was born. He'd save it, for now, knowing the guy had a lot on his plate.

He'd thought it was just Cambodia that had melted his heart enough to let her truly in, that had made him a little more carefree, but he figured out that last night in Cambodia, as he watched her cry, that it wasn't just Cambodia. It was her. She'd let herself open up and that had suckered him right into letting down his own guard. He'd understood better than she knew that her grief wasn't just about leaving all those people behind, it was leaving behind who they were there. Like people that went on vacation all the time, he'd hoped that he'd go back to his old self once he got home, but he knew that night that she was in his heart and she'd never go away.

Even though there were more direct flights to Singapore, he had deliberately asked Tanya to book the long way round to get to Cambodia. He wanted to drag the trip out, so he could spend more time with Roxie. He knew it wasn't very rational. Billionaires never traveled like that, and he wouldn't in normal circumstances. But he just couldn't help wanting to spend more time with

Roxie, even if the traveling was less than comfortable for him, and made her wanted to kill him. Part of him always seemed to enjoy winding Roxie up; when she was wound up, the Chloe inside of her came out.

She'd pirouetted her way into his heart a very long time ago, and had burrowed deeper during their time in the village. That was way too much for his liking, so he hadn't responded to that earlier text with anything other than a thumb pointing up.

Now, he was in his office, contemplating what to do with himself. He had to pull away from her somehow, without totally breaking the connection. He just wanted some space, not to walk away from her completely. He had to get his bearings somehow.

Kai called him and asked him to come up to New York for dinner. Lincoln was still exhausted from the trip but decided to go. Maybe a dose of his old life would remind him of why he needed to put up a wall that Roxie couldn't get past.

Tanya arranged a flight out an hour later and Lincoln raced home to pack some clothes and collect the keys to his apartment in New York. He didn't call Roxie or send her a message, he just left. It took some effort, but he ignored the pang of guilt he felt about that.

Kai picked him up at the airport and they went out to one of the top restaurants the city had to offer. He looked around at well-dressed men and women, all using impeccable manners to build the façade of polite society. Nobody spoke too loudly, or caused a scene, it was all self-control and few real laughs. Even the smiles seemed like facsimiles of the real thing. Lincoln remembered the way Roxie would laugh with the children in the village, or when she whispered with Chantou, and missed the sound.

Still, he made himself stay put. Love did not last, if it was ever real, and he needed to remind himself of that fact.

He went back to his apartment alone after dinner and stared out at the city below. It was here that he belonged, even if his heart wanted to be in Myrtle Beach. His jaw hardened as he sipped at a glass of bourbon. Somehow, he had to put Roxie at arm's length, had to get her out of his head.

Real-life meant that he had to be vigilant for threats, not only to her but to his business. He didn't have time for gallivanting around the globe or playing house. He had responsibilities, people counting on him.

Memories flooded into his brain and he closed his eyes, his free hand in the pocket of the black trousers he wore. The smile she'd worn every evening as she told him about her day, the way she laughed, the way she begged him to love her. That memory haunted him because he'd known, he'd seen it in her eyes, that she'd been asking for more than his body. She'd asked him for his heart, and he'd given it to her.

Until now.

He had to take it back. He didn't want to, he wanted to love her, have a life with her, maybe even create a family with her. But her name was Roxie now, not Chloe, and that meant she couldn't have a real place in his life. Not because she was a dancer or because she'd been a stripper, but because she was hiding. In trouble.

He wouldn't walk away from her, he decided. He'd give his very life for her if it came down to it, but he wouldn't give her his heart. That had to be his and only his.

He'd have to hide it somehow, protect it from her. She didn't deserve that, she deserved peace and happiness, deserved what they'd had in Cambodia, but he couldn't be the one to give it to her. Even if she became free of her past, he still wouldn't be able to give her what she deserved, not really.

He'd always be waiting for signs that she was bored with him, he'd always worry that she was tired of life with him and on the lookout for the next thrill, the man with more money. His brain rejected those thoughts. Roxie wasn't anything like this mother, but would she ever want to give up the life she lived now?

Those nights in Cambodia, that last night especially,

had proven that to him, but there was still that part of him that would not let the thoughts go.

Roxie loved excitement, thrived on danger, could make him beg for a moment of her attention with her skills. Would she really want to give that life up? A life that meant she didn't have to stay faithful to one man or woman, that meant she could explore whatever she wanted to, in exchange for the housecoats and baby diapers he could provide?

There were far too many doubts to let his heart run free, as had always been the case. He couldn't count on anything but himself. That's how it had always been and how it would always be. He couldn't stand to feel or experience the heartbreak he'd seen on so many of his former stepfathers' faces when his mother walked out on them. He couldn't let a woman break him like that. Ever.

He ended up staying in New York for three more days, just to prove to himself that he could do it. She called, texted him, but he kept the conversations short, always cutting her off mid-sentence to say he had to handle something, while he ignored some of her text messages. He knew she was getting upset by the third day, she hadn't called or texted him at all.

The first couple of days her voice had been happy, full of hope, but yesterday she sounded...defeated. He hated hearing that sound in her voice, hated how hopeless she sounded, but still, he'd interrupted her to end the call quickly.

He didn't want to be cruel to her, he didn't want to break her, but he had to do this to protect himself. From her.

It was the hardest thing he'd ever done. He had to stop himself from calling her a hundred times. He had to stop himself from boarding a plane and flying back to her. It was worse at night when he craved her scent, her touch, her voice, and those incredible eyes of hers. He'd taken a lot of cold showers over the last few days. He'd burned for her in his bed, alone at night, but he hadn't broken.

When he couldn't stand it anymore, he flew back to the beach. But even then, he didn't call her. He sat in his beach house alone, watching the waves crash against the sand as their time in the village replayed in his mind over and over again. He didn't go near his playroom at all, knowing he'd break if he did.

It wasn't fun, it was the most painful thing he'd ever put himself through. He missed every part of her, needed to be near her more than he'd ever needed anything else in his life, but he waited. He held his breath when the need threatened to overwhelm his own will, when he found his phone in his hand ready to call her.

It hurt that she stopped calling him, but he knew she

wasn't stupid. She'd know what he was doing and accept it. Whether she'd come to him when he did finally ask to see her remained to be seen. It was a chance he had to take.

Even if she refused to see him after this, he'd be able to keep an eye on her. He'd be able to protect her from the danger she was in, even if she never wanted to speak to him again. It would be worth losing her if it meant he'd get to watch her grow old.

And that was the crux of his current problem. He wanted to be the one that grew old with her. That couldn't happen though, he cared about her too much. He wanted too much from her and if his mother had taught him anything, it was that you couldn't count on forever.

He had to go through this overwhelming amount of pain now, he had to do this to them both, to protect himself. He smirked at his own thoughts, at his own sappiness. He'd never loved a woman. He thought now that what he'd felt for the girl she used to be was a kind of love, and he used that memory to remind himself countless times that no woman could hold a candle to her.

Now that he'd come to know Roxie, who that girl had become, he knew that no other woman would stand a chance of replacing her. But he'd have to find one he could keep at arm's length. Like the women at the restaurant tables in New York. If he ever decided to have a family, a wife, he'd pick one that he could keep at arm's length so that when she divorced him and tried to take his children away it wouldn't hurt so much.

He loved his mother, but she'd broken something inside of him a long time ago. She'd taken away his belief in fairy tales and dreams of being a knight in shining armor for some future princess. Even if that princess was named Chloe. Or Roxie, as the case may be.

He spent one more night alone, in a bed that now seemed far too big for him. He growled his way through work and drove himself home that evening with one thing on his mind. He'd waited long enough.

He needed her, needed to be inside of her, and he didn't care what he had to do to get it. He'd beg if he had to, he'd go to her if she demanded it. He'd let her tie him down in his playroom and whip him until she got rid of all the hurt and anger, he knew she had to be feeling.

It was a moment of weakness, he knew he should wait, that he wasn't where he needed to be yet to be able to hide his heart from her, but he couldn't wait anymore. He *needed* her more than he'd ever needed anything in his life. He physically hurt all over his body without her. He knew it wasn't a real sickness, a disease, that made him hurt like this, it was an emotional sickness that only she could cure.

He'd keep her at arm's length as long as he could, he

told himself, but he needed to taste her, desperately. His fingers punched in the words on his text messenger, his brain turned off when he hit send. He'd wait now and hope that she'd answer him.

He sat on his couch for an hour and waited, with no response from her.

Maybe she'd given up, maybe she was so hurt and angry that she wouldn't reply. Maybe it was best that she didn't. He got up, went to the bar cart where a bottle of bourbon waited for him, and filled a glass with two measures of the golden-brown liquid. His finger tapped against the glass and he walked into the kitchen to get some ice.

That's when he heard his doorbell and his heart thudded far too hard in his chest. She was here. Finally.

20

Roxie

She'd never known this kind of pain.

Or this kind of rejection.

It had taken her a while to catch on but when she did, pain crushed her, unlike anything she'd known before.

When they first got back from Cambodia, it took Roxie a few days to get over the sheer exhaustion of crossing the globe again. Her brain turned off that first night and it hadn't turned back on until she'd slept through two days. By the third day, she was ready to speak to other human beings again. She exchanged texts with everybody in the few moments she'd been awake over the last few days.

Wendy, Emily, and everybody else knew she was

back home but they all gave her the space to recover from the ordeal of getting back home. Even Lincoln had insisted she stay at her own place to recover. She'd wanted to stay with him, to maintain that closeness that she needed now.

She'd woken up and texted him, thinking about having a normal life with him, with a normal guy. A guy who loved her, like her parents had loved each other. She'd hoped for that with Nathan, but he proved her wrong. Lincoln wouldn't do that to her, though, not him.

When Lincoln barely responded to her text, she'd shrugged it off. When he barely spoke on the first call she made to him, she'd decided he was just still too tired to have a long conversation. The next day, she excused it all because maybe he was just having a hard time adjusting to this new thing between them.

The contract was over, but he didn't say anything about renewing it. Maybe that was a good thing?

There'd been a hundred thousand maybes swimming through her brain, so she sat alone in her hotel room. She'd gone out with Emily the day before, had her nails done, and bought some new lingerie to wear for Lincoln. Today she had a waxing appointment and the trickle of pain she felt as a tightness in her chest was completely murdered by the real pain of having her legs and nether regions waxed.

When he didn't come to her that night, when he didn't answer her calls, she sat alone in the dark. She knew this moment; she'd experienced it with Nathan.

He was tired of her.

The maybe-train started all over again.

Maybe she'd been too needy that last night in Cambodia.

Maybe Lincoln couldn't handle a real relationship.

What was it he'd said to her once? He couldn't maintain a platonic friendship with straight women, but he'd never had a real relationship with a woman.

He'd had a lot more than that from her and maybe that was just too much for him to handle.

When another day passed with no contact at all, she checked her bank account and decided that it was time to move on. He was done with her. She had enough to rent a new place for a while and maybe she should find her own vacation spot.

She lived at the beach, so she started to look at vacation rentals in the mountains of North Carolina. She could drive there and back. She could cry her heart out in solitude, where nobody would try to cheer her up. She could drive him out of her heart and out of her memory.

That was the lie she told herself anyway. She would never be able to completely get rid of Lincoln, there was a bond there that could never be forgotten. One that was stronger, much stronger than anything she'd ever had with Nathan or anyone else. She wasn't sure she'd even had this strong a bond with her own parents.

That had scared her at first, how much she felt like he'd become a part of her. She came to accept the fear and once she found herself back home, she'd hoped they could nourish that bond and bring it to life. That had been stupid of her though.

Lincoln was not the marrying kind. But then, neither was she.

She thought.

When she went out with Emily, they passed a bridal boutique and she stared at one dress, wanting it for her own. She smiled a smile that Emily nudged her over, but she put the thought away. It was too soon to be thinking of weddings and futures.

Sitting in a cabin a few days later, deep in the woods, covered in mosquito bites, Roxie hated herself for being a fool. It seemed her experience with Nathan hadn't taught her anything. And to be fair, Lincoln had warned her. He didn't want a wife, didn't want a relationship. He wanted sex and lots of it.

Well, she'd given him that plus some.

For a while, she'd known what it was like to be loved, she'd known what it was like to be loved by Lincoln Young in particular. It was beyond anything she'd ever known before. It had given her hope that there would be more, that they would be more. She expected to go through jet lag, maybe even reverse culture shock when she got home. It took her a couple of days to process coming back into her real world, but she'd done it.

She came out of her stupor with hope in her heart, with a heart that actually beat for someone else. There'd been plans, hopes that she wanted to get to right away, but Lincoln had stepped away.

She gave him space at the beginning, knowing his head was probably spinning as much as hers. But she knew he'd be alright in a few days. She knew he'd come for her. Only, he didn't. He'd taken a major step back from her.

What could have been a step into something totally new for them both had turned into something that nearly broke her. She rented the cabin and rushed up to hide away in her own feelings. The first night she startled at every sound, certain that somebody was about to kill her. She learned that the mountains could protect you, could encircle you in a sensation of safety, but they could also make you very, very afraid.

The second day she calmed down, opened the windows, and even went for a swim in the nearby lake. She went into town and had dinner on her own, and later went to bed, completely naked, too hot to even cover up with a sheet.

She'd barely been able to sleep for days, even before

she'd left Myrtle Beach. Her dreams replayed those nights with Lincoln in Cambodia, replayed how good it felt to be with him, and took it all a step further by producing a baby that could never be. That dream woke her up this morning with her heart racing and her heart breaking.

She wanted what she'd had with him in the past, wanted what her dreams told her could have been.

But now it seemed to be over. The chance to have those moments, that future, was gone.

She scratched at a particularly itchy mosquito bite and decided it was time to go home. She'd already spent two days in that hot cabin with a broken AC and accomplished nothing more than getting bit so many times it had at least distracted her. There was one bite she was certain was infected, but it was hidden by her shorts so she couldn't see it.

With a heavy heart, Roxie packed her bags and drove back home. It took much longer than she thought it would. By the time she got back to her hotel room, she was ready for bed, even though the sun had only just started to go down. She flopped down and fell asleep.

The next day she went out to meet up with Kitty and River. River was still with her couple, happy as she could be, but Kitty seemed quiet. Introspective.

Roxie tried to get more out of her, but both women kept trying to find out about her trip with Lincoln. She told them about the villagers, what she'd seen and heard, and how much she'd loved the country, but she couldn't talk about Lincoln.

"What happened? Do I need to stab him?" River asked, her eyes glued to Roxie's from the bench seat across the table.

Roxie smiled, put her hand over her friend's, and closed her eyes against the tears pricking her eyes. Once the tears had retreated, she opened them. "Nothing bad happened with him there. I promise, he was a complete gentleman. I just have some shit to deal with, that's all. It's nothing to do with him."

"If you're lying to us, we'll find out, Roxie," Kitty warned, her eyes picking apart Roxie's face. "And if he deserves a kicking, we'll be more than happy to give him one."

The fierceness in her eyes told Roxie that Kitty meant it.

"He doesn't deserve a kicking, at all." Even if he'd kicked her heart into dust. "It's fine, really."

"Mm-hmm." Both women mumbled and made Roxie laugh when they crossed their arms over their chests in tune with each other.

"Holy fuck, you two are turning into twins." Roxie laughed a little louder and sank back in her own seat. "I needed that laugh."

Both women looked concerned but didn't say

anything more.

Kitty left soon to teach a class and River left to rush off back to her couple. Roxie envied River that relationship, that need to be with her people. She felt the same need to be with Lincoln, but as the days passed, she started to think she'd never see him again. He hadn't said a word to her in three days at least. Maybe it was well and truly done and the possibility that she'd never see him at all again was very real.

She went back to her room, trying to decide whether to go to the theater to watch a movie or just go back to bed. Her phone buzzed, but she ignored it at first. It was probably Emily asking her to come over and see the baby, or another friend checking on her. She was fine, even if she was falling apart inside. She'd be okay and eventually she'd get over Lincoln. Somehow.

There was no way she'd force herself on him, even if she had caught herself driving to his house more than once since coming home. She wouldn't try to make him love her, or even be near her, if he didn't want to. Roxie Sinclair wasn't that kind.

Television bored her, movies didn't interest her, so she decided to read for a while. There was nothing else to do, that she wanted to do, so she picked up her phone. The screen was filled with notifications but only one interested her.

Lincoln Young had finally made contact.

"I need you."

That was all it said. That was all it needed to say.

She didn't care if it was desperate or not, she needed him too.

The old Roxie would have deleted the message, would have written him off, but she'd become someone new in Cambodia. Not a pushover, not that at all, but a woman who didn't push away what she needed. And what she needed more than anything was to be in his arms again.

It never occurred to her that he might need her to go shopping for him, or something along those lines. Lincoln would not have written the word 'need' if he didn't mean that he needed her for herself. He'd have typed out that he wanted her to go buy his groceries or pick up his dry cleaning. No, the word need meant he'd cracked and wanted her to be with him. At last.

For a moment she considered going over in jeans and a t-shirt. Or the pajama short set she'd changed into when she came back to her room. That wouldn't do. If she was going to see him, she wanted some kind of armor on, and lingerie had always been her armor.

She washed her hair, curled it alluringly, added makeup to her face, and then put on the new lingerie she'd bought. It was a purple and black ensemble that consisted of an empire-waist babydoll, tiny black thong panties, and the garters and stockings that he loved to look at. She put a short-sleeved black coatdress over top, added some black heels, and checked herself in the mirror.

The old Roxie stared back at her, and somewhere beneath that woman was the girl named Chloe that she used to be. On top of them both were the eyes of the new woman Lincoln had taught her to be. A woman that had hope in the gentle smile on her lips, who had love that burned out of her crystal blue eyes. Roxie felt tears prick for the thousandth time but blinked them away and pulled her lips in to fight the pain.

She'd go to him, take what he could give her, and somehow, *somehow*, she'd make that be enough. And if she couldn't, then she'd do them both a favor and walk away. But she needed this one last moment with him. If he told her he didn't want her when she got there, at least she'd know for sure that it was done. It was a chance she'd take.

But he'd typed the word need.

That meant so much more than want. That meant so much more than get. He needed her. The man he was when he first walked back into her life had no needs. He had wants, yes, but needs? No.

With nervous fingers, she got into her car, kicked off her heels so she could drive, and started the engine. Traffic was a nightmare, but it wasn't anything unusual in the summer here. She dealt with it and before she knew it, she was staring at his open security gate. He didn't leave it open often, but maybe he was in such a hurry he decided to leave it open for her.

She drove up, parked behind his car, and pulled down the visor to check her makeup. Everything was as it should be, so she got out of the car but stopped to lean back against the door. Should she go in there? Was this a stupid thing to do?

What if he slept with her then walked out on her again?

But what if tonight changed everything? What if he asked her to stay?

She walked up to the door, at last, opening the buttons of her dress, and hit the doorbell. With breath held, she waited, a smile plastered on her face. The door opened and a woman stared out at her. Roxie blinked, her brain confused seeing it wasn't Lincoln's face but a much older version of a face that was as familiar as her own.

"Chloe?" The woman asked after a long moment of staring at her.

Roxie frowned, the world tilting over suddenly. The voice was familiar too.

"June?"

Lincoln's sister. Why was Lincoln's sister here?

* * *

DARK DESIRES
~ A billionaire dark romance series ~
Dark Desire
Dark Rules
Dark Secret
Dark Time
Dark Truth

BARRE TO BAR
~ A billionaire second chance series ~
Dancing With Lies
Dancing With Temptation
Dancing With Doubt
Dancing With Guilt
Dancing With Redemption

TWISTED INTENTION
~ A billionaire revenge romance series ~
Twisted Beauty
Twisted Love
Twisted Fate

Mafia's Obsession
~ A hot mafia romance series ~
Mafia's Dirty Secret
Mafia's Fake Bride
Mafia's Final Play

Screaming Demons
~ An MC romance series full of suspense ~
Rough Start
Rough Ride
Rough Choice
Rough Patch
Rough Return
Rough Road
Rough Trip
Rough Night
Rough Love

Standalone Contemporary Romance
Billionaire in Vegas
Billionaire Hunt

Billionaire's Game
Billionaire Retreat
Billionaire On Air
A Chance To Love
Somebody To Love
Not Mine To Love

Check out Summer's entire collection at
www.summercooper.com/books

ABOUT SUMMER COOPER

Thank you so much for reading. Without you, it wouldn't be possible for me to be a full-time author. I hope you enjoy reading my books as much as I do writing them.

Besides (obviously!) reading and writing, I also love cuddling my dogs, shouting at Alexa, being upside down (aka Yoga) and driving my family cray-cray!

Get in touch at
hello@summercooper.com
www.summercooper.com

facebook.com/summercooperauthor
instagram.com/summercooperauthor
goodreads.com/summercooper
bookbub.com/profile/summer-cooper